From Up Here

by Liz Flahive

SAMUEL FRENCH

FOUNDED 1830

NEW YORK HOLLYWOOD LONDON TORONTO

· SAMUELFRENCH.COM

ISBN 978-0-573-66325-3   Printed in U.S.A.   #8235

IMPORTANT BILLING AND CREDIT REQUIREMENTS

All producers of *FROM UP HERE* must give credit to the Author of the Play in all programs distributed in connection with performances of the Play, and in all instances in which the title of the Play appears for the purposes of advertising, publicizing or otherwise exploiting the Play and/or a production. The name of the Author *must* appear on a separate line on which no other name appears, immediately following the title and *must* appear in size of type not less than fifty percent of the size of the title type.

Originally produced by the Manhattan Theatre Club, Lynne Meadow, Artistic Director, Barry Grove, Executive Producer, Daniel Sullivan, Acting Artistic Director 2007-08 Season in association with Ars Nova on March 27, 2008.

MANHATTAN THEATRE CLUB
New York City Center Stage I

Artistic Director
LYNNE MEADOW

Executive Producer
BARRY GROVE

Acting Artistic Director 2007-08 Season
DANIEL SULLIVAN

In association with
ARS NOVA

Presents

FROM UP HERE

By
LIZ FLAHIVE

with

JENNI BARBER   **ARIJA BAREIKIS**   **AYA CASH**
BRIAN HUTCHISON   **WILL ROGERS**   **TOBIAS SEGAL**
JOEL VAN LIEW   **JULIE WHITE**

Scenic Design
ALLEN MOYER

Costume Design
MATTIE ULLRICH

Lighting Design
PAT COLLINS

Sound Design
JILL BC DuBOFF

Original Music
TOM KITT

Production Stage Manager
DAVID H. LURIE

Casting
DAVID CAPARELLIOTIS

Directed by
LEIGH SILVERMAN

General Manager
FLORIE SEERY

Associate Artistic
Director/Production
MANDY GREENFIELD

Director of Marketing
DEBRA A. WAXMAN

Press Representatives
BONEAU/BRYAN-BROWN

Production Manager
KURT GARDNER

Director of Casting
NANCY PICCIONE

Director of Development
JILL TURNER LLOYD

Special thanks to the Harold and Mimi Steinberg Charitable Trust for supporting new American plays and musicals at Manhattan Theatre Club. Manhattan Theatre Club wishes to express its appreciation to Theatre Development Fund for its support of this production.

CHARACTER LIST

KENNY - 17

LAUREN - 15, his sister

GRACE - 41, his mother

DANIEL - 32, his step-father

CAROLINE - 32, his aunt

CHARLIE - 17, a high school senior

KATE - 17, a high school senior

MR. GOLDBERGER - 40, a guidance counselor

OFFICER STEVENS - 40, a police officer

NOTE: The role of Officer Stevens should be played by the same actor that plays Mr. Goldberger.

NOTE: The / in the dialogue scores the specific moment where the next line should begin overlapping.

If the direction (overlapping) is given, lines should just be spoken right over the next.

SPECIAL THANKS

To Jenny Gersten for forcing me to finish and to Evan Cabnet for steering the first reading.

The wild bunch at Ars Nova: Jason Eagan, Emily Shooltz, Jon Steingart, Jenny Weiner and Kim Rosenstock couldn't have been more stalwart in their support.

To everyone at Manhattan Theater Club, particularly Mandy Greenfield, Dan Sullivan and Barry Grove. I am so grateful for the enormous leap of faith—and for our high-class production.

Thanks to Julie, Brian, Arija, Tobias, Aya, Jenni, Will and Joel for all their energy, humor and compassion. Also, Matthew Stadelmann, Talia Balsam and Samantha Mathis gave generously of their time and talent every time we asked. Thanks to Dave for his infinite patience and casting genius.

To Allen for the kitchen, Jill for the gusty wind, Pat for the late afternoon sunlight, Tom for the kickass love song and David for all manner of peace-keeping.

Leigh Silverman knew exactly where to push and pull me along. Without her, I would have gone right off the road.

To Frank Pugliese, Willie Reale and everyone at the 52nd St. Project for reading, talking and making me write.

Thanks and love to Jeff, for all of it.

This play is for my parents. And for my sister.

THE POSTCARD

*(Spotlight on **KENNY**, barely holding an enormous bag of dog food. Swirling wind gusts as **CAROLINE** drops in from above wearing full climbing gear, strapped into a climbers harness connected to a rope.)*

CAROLINE. Kenny! This is Katenga! *(Grabs the rope tightly)* I'm convinced everyday that I'm going to fall to my death! But then, here I am, looking out from a forgotten summit. A forgotten summit. That's what my guide Ron told me. I told Ron not to romanticize things; I'd seen three Chuckles wrappers and a condom on the way up and litter is one of the first signs of mass tourism. But, my point is: Today. Today will be a good one, Kenny. I'll be there if I can. But you know, if I'm not, stare right at this picture and think about me thinking about you. Up here, the wind burn hits your cheek so hard it almost feels hot. A warm smack of air right in the face, thousands of feet above the ground. Postcards are too small to hold all the things I want to say to you. No room for anything anymore. Not even my name. *(To herself, looking out, smiling, happily)* Goddammit!

(A strong gust of wind sounds and pulls Caroline out of view as lights rise on)

THE KITCHEN

(Early morning. DANIEL sits at the table with coffee and the paper. We hear dogs barking offstage.)

DANIEL. It's like a little duet.

KENNY. ...What?

DANIEL. Your dogs don't like to bark together. They like to solo. They've been doing it for an hour. It's the yippy one and then low bark low bark. Yip yip. LOW. LOW LOW. Yip Yip Yip. LOW. And then they pause. And then again. One. Then the other. It's awesome. Muffin?

KENNY. No.

DANIEL. Where you taking that?

KENNY. Uh... outside. Mom hates the smell.

DANIEL. We can put it in the basement.

KENNY. No/ that's okay.

(LAUREN enters, wearing jeans and her bra.)

DANIEL. Good morning! Did you forget something?

LAUREN. No. Did you?

DANIEL. Nope. *(Pats his chest)* My clothes are all here.

LAUREN. My blue shirt... That was at the cleaners. / Mom said that you picked it up...

DANIEL. Ohhhh. I forgot to pick up the dry cleaning.

LAUREN. Daniel. Seriously. People notice how many times I wear something. I plan my rotations a week in advance.

(KENNY grabs the dog bowls off the counter, struggles with the bag. It rips a little and spills a trail of kibble.)

DANIEL. You can still wear something.

LAUREN. I'm trying to do my best. *(beat)* Can you help him or/ something?

KENNY. I got it.

LAUREN. Yeah. You're getting it/ everywhere.

DANIEL. I'll take/ it.

KENNY. I got/ it.

LAUREN. You got it all over/ the floor.

DANIEL. Lauren, pick up those nuggets before/ someone steps on them. Kibble. Whatever, just up. Up.

KENNY. Kibble/.

LAUREN. It smells like a barn in here!

DANIEL. Hey, *(taps his knees)* use your knees. Makes it easier. *(beat)* Bend em. (**KENNY** *does.*) What is that. Twenty? Fifteen?

KENNY. ...Uh, thirty. Maybe.

DANIEL. That's good for a kid your size. Got some muscles hiding in those arms.

KENNY. ...I guess.

DANIEL. You lift?

KENNY. *(Struggling)* ... I'm lifting this.

DANIEL. You working out?

KENNY. *(About to drop it)* Uh. No... I gotta...

(**KENNY** *exits. Fast.* **LAUREN** *pours herself some coffee and sits down.*)

LAUREN. *(Annoyed/Bored by whatever's coming next.)* What.

DANIEL. You drink coffee now?

LAUREN. I drink lots of things. Tea. Coffee.

DANIEL. Kenny doesn't.

LAUREN. We're not twins. He won't drink dark liquids. He has a whole thing about it.

DANIEL. When I was fifteen, I drank juice. And I grew 8 inches in one year.

LAUREN. I love being small. Most people can pick me up.

DANIEL. You don't want to get big and strong?

LAUREN. Yeah, I totally want to be a big strong girl. That'd be so exciting.

DANIEL. It will be exciting when you get really hearty and we can harness you to a sleigh and you can drive all the neighborhood children around in the snow while they sing.

(KENNY enters, his leg is bleeding.)

LAUREN. Do you, like, write down what you're going to say to me the night before? Because that's what you sound like sometimes.

DANIEL. Don't you find maintaining this level of sarcasm exhausting?

LAUREN. That wasn't sarcastic… Kenny. What happened?

KENNY. I dunno.

LAUREN. Yes yes you do./ That's blood. That's your bleeding leg. What did you do?

DANIEL. Sit down, here, we/ should elevate it. I think. Let me look.

KENNY. It's not that… it's alright, /*(Inhales sharply)*

DANIEL. Oh that's not good… Here we should…

LAUREN. No! He could have rabies! RABIES!/ Don't touch it.

DANIEL. Have they had their shots?

KENNY. Yeah.

LAUREN. Rabies /shots?

KENNY. Yeah, rabies /shots.

DANIEL. *(Forcefully)* Hey! Hold this on it, hold this.

LAUREN. Dogs aren't people, you asshole. *(urgently, almost letting on that she's worried)* He's really/ bleeding a lot.

DANIEL. You need put pressure on it. /Look, feel that? Pressure.

KENNY. *(Gritting his teeth)* I got it.

LAUREN. And stop spending all your time sitting around in that pen with them. It's/ sad.

DANIEL. Lauren. Go find a god damn shirt.

(LAUREN exits)

LAUREN. *(on her way offstage)* MOM! DANIEL DIDN'T PICK UP THE DRYCLEANING.

DANIEL. Great… She's gonna get out the bleach and it's gonna be/ a whole production. Stand on… *(rifles through the sections sorting what he wants to read and what* *he has read.)* Here. Bleed all over the travel section.

KENNY. I'm supposed to separate them when I feed them. Rodney sees Dingo's food and he wants it too so…

DANIEL. Hey. Tough it out. *(beat)* Gotta make it to your first day back.

KENNY. …Yeah.

> *(GRACE enters, hair damp, shirt unbuttoned with her bra exposed. From the waist down she's completely pulled together, shoes, pants, the works.)*

GRACE. What happened?!

DANIEL. He's fine.

GRACE. He's been /mauled.

KENNY. It's just blood.

GRACE. Let me see, is it deep?

KENNY. I got in the way. It was my fault/.

DANIEL. It's no one's fault/. Baby. Can you back up over… there… please?

GRACE. *(Backing up very slightly)* That looks deep. He has to be seen by someone./ A doctor.

DANIEL. It's nothing. **(GRACE** *shoots him a look)* It'll clot right up. C'mon, /he's a bruiser.

KENNY. Mom. It's fine. See. *(He takes the towel off, shows her quickly.)*

GRACE. *(Hugging him tightly)* I should have said no to that second dog.

KENNY. Okayokay….get off me… *(Pushes her away)*

GRACE. *(Buttoning her shirt)* I'm the first woman you ever saw topless. You remember that.

> **(DANIEL** *looks up at* **KENNY** *and shakes his head slightly, as if to say, don't remember that, checks out his leg.)*

DANIEL. Hey, it's stopped. Almost.

GRACE. Oh. Did blood get in the grout?… You know what. It's fine. The floor guy is coming on Tuesday to do the entire downstairs. This place is going to look fantastic, we'll be able to sell it in a second. *(Beat)* So? Now?

(DANIEL nods. She exits, excited.) LAUREN!! We're giving your brother his PRESENTS!!

(DANIEL hands KENNY a lunch. KENNY! is written on it in colored marker.)

DANIEL. Made you lunch.

KENNY. Oh. I don't want anything./ It's not...

DANIEL. Hey. Double chips in there. And a note.

KENNY. You put a note in my lunch?

DANIEL. It's a special day.

KENNY. It's not. It's Monday.

DANIEL. Everyone's... Your dad sent you that check and you got that postcard the other day from your Aunt Caroline. From India or something.

KENNY. Nepal. Don't put notes in my lunch.

(GRACE reenters holding a large black case with a big red bow and her camera)

GRACE. And this! This is from me. And Daniel. And Lauren.

(KENNY looks at her. He opens the case. Looks at it. Looks at GRACE. Looks at it.)

KENNY. It's a saxophone.

GRACE. Yes!

KENNY. It's a saxophone.

GRACE. It's a saxophone. For Marching Band. I called up and told Mrs. Hankins how interested you were in music and discipline.

KENNY. No. I'm not...

GRACE. You said/ you...

KENNY. When did I say that?

GRACE. Remember? We were at Dr. Marish's office. We talked about it for the whole session. All the things you'd want to maybe try and get involved in?

KENNY. Maybe get involved. You signed me up?

GRACE. Well, you can sit in. Listen to rehearsals. Practice marching.

KENNY. *(He picks up the sax to look at it.)* I don't…

GRACE. Oh! That's great!… Pick it up. Oh. Stay right there. *(Gets out her camera)* Move to the left, I'm getting a glare.

KENNY. I don't even know/ how to…

DANIEL. Why don't we do this outside in the front yard near that really nice tree?

KENNY. No. No. Here's good.

(**KENNY** *reluctantly picks up the sax.*)

LAUREN. *(as she enters)* What's that?

KENNY. It's/ a saxophone.

GRACE. It's from you too.

LAUREN. It is not/.

GRACE. Oh! That's it. *(Picture)* Hold it to the side, I can't see your face. Why don't you pretend to play it? Like a real jazz man.

KENNY. No.

(**GRACE** *takes the second picture. Big flash.* **LAUREN** *hands him a small package.*)

GRACE. It's so curvy, isn't it. Like a golden little woman.

(**KENNY** *opens* **LAUREN**'s *gift, almost smiles.*)

GRACE. Well? What is it?

LAUREN. It's a slingshot.

GRACE. Cute. That/ stays here.

LAUREN. You're/ welcome.

KENNY. Thank you. *(Looks at Grace.)* Thanks. For the/ saxophone.

GRACE. You're welcome. It'll be great, don't you think? How's your speech coming? Is it finished

KENNY. Yeah… Almost.

GRACE. I need to see it before/ you…

KENNY. It's not done.

GRACE. How much have you written?

KENNY. I wrote out a page.

GRACE. Neatly?

LAUREN. Why does that matter.

DANIEL. *(Hands* **LAUREN** *her lunch.)* Here./

GRACE. So you have a whole page?

KENNY. Yeah. And it's neat.

DANIEL. Why don't we order in tomorrow night? A big pizza. A little audience. You can practice saying it// in front of…

LAUREN. *(To* **GRACE***)* I gotta go. I'm taking the bus.

KENNY. *(To* **DANIEL***)* I don't want to practice right now.

GRACE. *(Overlapping, to* **LAUREN***)*The bus? Since when do you take the bus?

DANIEL. *(Overlapping)* You have to say it outloud at some point so you're more comfortable/ when you…

LAUREN. *(Overlapping, to* **GRACE***)* I'm trying new things.

KENNY. *(Overlapping)* Yeah. I don't really think that'll…

GRACE. *(Overlapping, to* **LAUREN***)* I'm driving Kenny in a few minutes, I can take you too.

LAUREN. No. I want to… *(to* **KENNY***)* I'll see you at lunch. Okay? I don't want to get there with/ all the…

KENNY. Yeah. It's okay.

LAUREN. /Okay.

GRACE. Hey. Look at me. Are you pulling out your hair again?

LAUREN. Uh. No.

GRACE. Didn't you wear that shirt yesterday?

LAUREN. *(Shoots* **DANIEL** *a look)* I'm not pulling out my hair.

GRACE. I keep finding little clumps of hair. In /your bathroom.

LAUREN. *(Exiting)* Hair falls out, okay?/ God… !

GRACE. *(Calling after her.)* Are there even seatbelts on the bus?

*(***LAUREN** *exits to the bus stop.* **GRACE** *sighs, exits to finish drying her hair.)*

DANIEL. That was nice, huh? *(Pause)* So. We should go

through this. Before you leave. Together.

(DANIEL *begins sorting through Kenny's backpack and logging every item on an inventory sheet. A pause.*)

DANIEL. *(a little forced)* Lauren was telling me you won't drink dark liquids.

KENNY. Yeah.

DANIEL. *(sorting through things)* Never?

KENNY. Nope.

DANIEL. Wow. *(beat)* I hate eggs. They make me break out into a sweat. The way the middles are either all... *(shudders)* I can't talk about it. What's your deal? With the drinks?

KENNY. Uh, they usually, like, leave a film. On your tongue. And I need to... see the glass or cup. The inside of it.

DANIEL. Oh.

KENNY. To see what I'm doing.

DANIEL. Sure. Awareness. I gotcha.

(DANIEL *takes a very sharpened pencil out of the bag*)

KENNY. ...It's a /pencil...

DANIEL. You have pens. Right?

KENNY. I can't do any real shading with a pen.

DANIEL. Stick with pens and we'll see how this week goes. Maybe you could try out for Lacrosse or something?

KENNY. Mom doesn't want me doing anything where I have to run anywhere or hit anyone for fun.

(A doorbell rings.)

DANIEL. *(Repacking the backpack for Kenny)* Well, then marching band's gonna be just the thing. *(Calling offstage)* GRACE! CAN YOU GET THAT? Listen. You can take your sketchbook. Just watch what you put in there.

(A doorbell rings.)

KENNY. It's my book.

DANIEL. Yeah. So watch it. Because everyone else is. GRAAACE! DOOR!

KENNY. I'll get/ it.

DANIEL. No. I'll get it. Here.

(DANIEL *signs the inventory sheet, exits.* KENNY *signs the sheet.*)

DANIEL. *(offstage, quietly)* Sorry, no, he's in the kitchen.

CAROLINE. *(offstage/whispering)* Up here?

DANIEL. *(entering)* No. Over here. *(To* KENNY*)* Hey! You're never going to/ believe who's here to see you!

(CAROLINE *enters wearing an enormous backpack.*)

CAROLINE. God! Who taught you how you surprise some-one. *(Sees Kenny's face)* Oh. See that. That's surprised.

DANIEL. Uh. It's your aunt!/ Surprise!

KENNY. I know.

CAROLINE. I told you I'd maybe make/ it here in time to…

DANIEL. So you knew about this?

KENNY. Sort of, but /it's… Aunt Caroline.

CAROLINE. Look at that face. You didn't think I'd actually show. Honestly, I didn't either. Four different planes, the odds of not dying were like 14 to 2. The tiniest one had these toothpick propellers and the whole way it was Ooooooooooh shiiiiiiiiiiiiiit. The luggage was too much for it so we took out all our non-essentials and left them in a box on the runway. But I managed to get these on. *(Hands him something rolled up in newspaper)*. I wrapped em.

(KENNY *unwraps some really rustic looking colored pencils.*)

DANIEL. You got him sticks?

CAROLINE. Yes. I got/ him sticks.

KENNY. They're colored pencils.

CAROLINE. This ancient man I met in Bangalore makes them by hand, it takes forever/ and I sat there for an hour and watched him finish that blue one…

GRACE. *(Entering, dressed for work, rummaging through her bag for her keys)* There's a terrible sound coming from the pipe in the upstairs bathroom it's like a... *(sees her sister, stops cold).*

DANIEL. *(beat)* Surprise!

GRACE. *(Recovers and turns it on.)* Oh my god! It is!

(A slight pause)

KENNY. ...It's Aunt Caroline/... !

GRACE. I know! It's incredible, did you just get here?

CAROLINE. This morning,/ yeah.

GRACE. I had no idea you'd... and oh, did you meet?/ This is Daniel!

CAROLINE. Yeah, I know. He let me in.

GRACE. You have to go change those pants.

KENNY. Fine. /

(KENNY Exits)

CAROLINE. What happened?

GRACE. He's fine.

DANIEL. Wow. *(beat. Looks at them.)* You have the same nose.

CAROLINE. *(pleased)* I did not tell him to say that. *(To* **DANIEL***)* Fucked up, isn't it.

DANIEL. It's crazy./ I can't stop staring at them.

GRACE. It's not that crazy. We are related. *(To* **CAROLINE***)* If I'd known, we could have picked you up from the airport.

CAROLINE. Honestly, it was all so last minute. I was in the middle of this 24 day trek and I didn't know if I'd get it together to get a flight but then the real shock! I actually did! *(beat)* I should have called first.

DANIEL. Why? It's no big deal, we have room. Put your bag/ upstairs in the...

CAROLINE. I'm not staying here.

GRACE. Oh./ Okay.

CAROLINE. No, I mean, I'm camping. There's that gorgeous spot up in Hawthorne next to the forest preserve / that's...

GRACE. Well, that's nice.

CAROLINE. Shit. I'm sorry I didn't call ahead. So you could plan.

GRACE. No. No! It's fine. Just... we're running late but it's such a surprise that you came... *(Gives her an awkward hug, since she's still wearing her backpack.)* Hi.

(KENNY Re-Enters)

CAROLINE. Oh. Hi. Thanks. No, it's cool, he's gotta go. *(Gives KENNY a little nudge toward the door.)* Don't be tardy.

KENNY. Yeah...

GRACE. *(To DANIEL)* Do you have my keys? *(noticing, To KENNY)* Excuse me. What are those? You can't take sharp sticks/ to school.

KENNY/CAROLINE. They're not sticks/They're colored pencils.

DANIEL. *(To himself.)* Leave the pencils. Take the cannolli. *(They all look at him)* Sorry. Sorry. Aren't they in your purse?

GRACE. No, I already looked there. *(To KENNY)* Do you have everything? *(KENNY nods, zipping up his bag, putting on his sweatshirt.)* Where's my... *(puts her hand on top of her head and feels her glasses. Keeps looking around.)* Oh. Okay. She forgot her... I don't understand why your sister wanted to take the bus.

KENNY. Guys take the bus to get blow jobs from girls on the way to school.

GRACE. Excuse me?

KENNY. Some guys take the/ bus to get blow jobs...

GRACE. Daniel... please... can you...

DANIEL. *(amused/intrigued)* Kenny, I am sure/ that's not why she's taking the bus.

GRACE. How can you say that?/ That's, she's... she's your sister!

KENNY. No, that's not... it's just something that happens...

DANIEL. He's gonna/ be late if you don't...

GRACE. *(raises her voice)* This is very hard for her, too. Do you think it's easy for her,/ right now?

KENNY. No… I don't know.

GRACE. *(Lowers her voice. Calm authority.)* Go get in the car. Now. I'll be right there.

(KENNY exits.)

CAROLINE. I'm going to pretend to go to the bathroom for a minute.

GRACE. It's through the door on/ the left.

CAROLINE. I remember.

(CAROLINE exits. DANIEL grabs GRACE and gives her a hug.)

GRACE. Oh my god. You're one of those people who likes surprises aren't you.

DANIEL. Come on,/it's nice that she… Grace. You've gotta breathe.

GRACE. He's barely gotten back on a schedule and… I am breathing.

DANIEL. Look, the therapist made a good point about getting us into yoga. We don't have to do it together. But I think we should make it something we all do as a family. Separately.

GRACE. *(Looking for the keys)* I know, I know, we should.

DANIEL. And I realize last night was bad timing on top of everything else. I don't know what it is but after I come, all I want to do is make plans and talk about the future.

GRACE. That used to be one of my favorite things about you.

DANIEL. Really?

GRACE. Yes. But now my favorite thing about you is how you understand that I'm not having a baby so you can stay at home with it and find yourself. Dammit. I swear/ I put them in here.

DANIEL. *(reaching for her purse)* Here. *(taking it)* C'mon, you know I'll find them faster. *(While he looks.)* What I

should have said last night is that I'd like you to give
it some serious consideration. And I should have left
it at that instead of going into that list of my favorite
girl's names and... *(beat)* But I think it'd be/ good for
all of us.

GRACE. Fine. I'll think about it. I will. Alright?/ Are they...

(CAROLINE *walks back in, unseen.*)

DANIEL. *(Pulls the keys out of the bag and holds them above his
head triumphant)* You'll think about it because... I AM
THE KEYMASTER.

GRACE. *(Grabs the keys. Kisses him.)* I don't know how you do
that. *(Kisses him again. Remembers)* Shit. I didn't make
the/ bed.

DANIEL. Go. I've got it.

(GRACE *exits.*)

CAROLINE. Looks like it's you and me, new guy...

DANIEL. Yeah. *(beat)* I'm not really new. Anymore. To them.
I guess a year is still newly married. I mean, it seems
like I've been here forever. To me. *(beat)* Hey, are you
hungry? Or can I get you some water or...

CAROLINE. Do you have any beer? Bud Light? Even if it's
warm...

DANIEL. It's what, almost 8:30? I can go, uh... get some?

CAROLINE. Nonono. I just I like to drink the crappy American stuff whenever I have the chance.

DANIEL. The Peace Corps denies you bad domestic beer?

CAROLINE. The one real drawback. You have juice?

DANIEL. Juice. Yeah. *(Goes to get her juice)* I went to work for
Habitat For Humanity right after college. And I came
back after a week.

CAROLINE. Well, it's not for everyone.

DANIEL. Yeah. It all worked out in the end. I got a job at
this tea shop at the mall. Which led me to a bunch of
other jobs. At the mall.

CAROLINE. Didn't you meet Grace at the mall?

DANIEL. Yeah. Never figured managing a Pottery Barn would actually change my life. Orange okay?

CAROLINE. That's fine. *(beat)* I loved everything about it. The minute I joined. But I miss a lot of stuff. Birthdays, funerals, *(Gesturing to him)* weddings.

DANIEL. Well, it's great that you're here now. I haven't seen Kenny this happy… ever.

CAROLINE. Really. That was happy? Man, what'd you do to him?

DANIEL. Uhm, I didn't do… /anything.

CAROLINE. His eyes are so glassy and he's sorta… *(makes the flatline noise).*

DANIEL. He's on a serious amount of Paxil for a thirty pound kid. It's this drug that…

CAROLINE. I know what Paxil is./ I don't live in a hole.

DANIEL. Sorry. Right. That was/… I'm sorry.

CAROLINE. Whoa, no, I'm sorry. I bang down your door, piss off your wife, demand beer and *(smells, smells inside her shirt)* God, and I stink! *(Takes off her shirt and rummages through her bag to get a new shirt.)* I mean, he was always quiet. But he would look at people when they talked to him. And when he was concentrating on something, he would hum. These weird dramatic little tunes. He smiled. I think. Maybe not all the time but it wasn't infrequent. I'm definitely going to start wearing actual deodorant. Something synthetic and powdery. Like Secret. Or Degree. *(Puts on a new shirt)* That for me?

DANIEL. *(Looks at the glass)* Oh. *(beat)* Yes. *(Hands it to her)*

CAROLINE. *(She drinks it.)* It smells nice in here. Like real lemons or something. What is that?

DANIEL. I… I started making my own potpourri. I took this class. Grace kept buying the kind that smelled Christmasy. Cinnamon. Cloves.

CAROLINE. *(A beat. Then, genuine)* Wow. /Good for you.

DANIEL. Yeah, well, it's not hard. How long are you staying?

CAROLINE. I don't know. Why? You think I should leave.

DANIEL. No! Everyone's glad you're here. *(beat)* Really. She is. It's just a stressful day, you know she hates surprises and we're trying to have a baby/ so it's…

CAROLINE. She's pregnant?/ That's crazy!

DANIEL. Well we're trying…

CAROLINE. That's big news! Has she/started telling…?

DANIEL. It'll be unreal.

CAROLINE. Yeah. Unreal. *(beat)* Did this house get bigger?

DANIEL. We knocked out that weird half-wall.

CAROLINE. It feels different./Wider.

DANIEL. You like it?

CAROLINE. It's awesome. God, I haven't been in an actual house in years. *(beat)* So, you'll give me a ride over? To the campgrounds? *(Putting the backpack on)* I want to get a good spot for my tent.

DANIEL. Is that everything?

CAROLINE. This is it.

DANIEL. *(A little awestruck)* That's great. I always wanted one of those big packs. It seems so cool. Just strap everything I own onto my back, grow a beard and go hike something. *(beat)* You get tired of carrying it?

CAROLINE. Oh I don't even feel it anymore.

DANIEL. Yeah? It's not heavy?

CAROLINE. Oh, it's heavy but honestly, man, I can walk for miles… .

(She grins. Lights out. Lights up on…)

THE BUS STOP

(LAUREN and KATE waiting at the bus stop, stage left. They're not waiting together, they're just at the same stop.

KATE is listening to her ipod listening to music, not paying attention to anyone.

After a minute, CHARLIE walks up and stands and waits. He looks at LAUREN.)

CHARLIE. You're a sophomore, right? Kenny Barrett's sister? *(She nods. beat)* Charlie. *(beat)* Senior. *(beat)* You going to the dance on Friday?

(She looks at him. Ignores him. A pause)

CHARLIE. People say you fucked two guys at Kristi Shinnick's party last weekend? Did you know people are saying that?

(A pause. They stand there. No bus.)

CHARLIE. David Blitzstein said the minute he put it in you, you started crying. Did he hurt you?

(A beat. They stand there. No bus.)

CHARLIE. Because it's only supposed to hurt the first time. I mean, it's not like I know, but I do because I talk to girls and they tell me stuff like, well not exactly what happens. I don't press for details because it's private – it's not that but I have close girl friends, not girlfriends but we talk about sex. Not just about sex but it's well, it's topical. Mostly sex is just topical, it's not paramount, not yet, anyway, because it's all just started or not started or not that good but, I guess it's safe to assume it will become a serious variable. At some point. But sex is not the most important thing and I think a lot of people feel compelled to decide what that most important thing is, especially right now. I don't understand it, ordering the importance of everything. Like how everyone's all obsessed with class rank, who's number 20, who's right up next to you at 19.

And fine, I think it's good to know where you stand and but it's like everyone is so hung up on trying to get the least important things to matter the most. Whatever. But, see, I love walking around, knowing what I want. That's actually useful. To think about something, and really want it. And then you see it and knowing it actually exists is... It's this feeling like I'm looking at everything through one of those cardboard tubes, the ones that hold paper towels and everything's all... *(makes a circle with both his hands and extends one out like a handheld telescope)* And I know what I want is to stand next to you and talk to you. Here I am. Doing exactly what I want. So this. Yeah. This is such a great day. Already. And it's pretty early. *(beat)* Hey. *(beat)* Bus.

(They all look at the approaching bus. Lights fade on the bus stop. A school bell rings as lights rise on)

THE LUNCHROOM

(KENNY sits at the end of a cafeteria table sketching in a big black book. There are two brown lunch bags and his saxophone laid out next to him. LAUREN comes up, looks around as she sits down next to him.)

KENNY. You forgot this.

(He hands her the other lunch.)

KENNY. Aunt Caroline's here.

LAUREN. When did that happen?

KENNY. After you left.

(LAUREN pulls apart her sandwich)

LAUREN. I thought she was on a mountain somewhere or… Ugh. Look! Mayonnaise. On both pieces of bread.

KENNY. Daniel likes mayonnaise./ So what.

LAUREN. He's so excessive. *(She wipes the bread clean on the paper bag)* Oh my god. Someone's been writing about you in the girl's bathroom. Seriously. Facebook that shit. It's totally Melanie Russell. She didn't even spell psycho right. So I wrote underneath it, "Melanie Russell has syphilis and no one will ever fuck her." And some evil symbol I made up.

KENNY. Thanks a/ lot.

LAUREN. She was on the list wasn't she? *(beat)* Whatever. Everyone has a list in their head. /You just wrote yours down.

KENNY. It wasn't an organized list.

LAUREN. *(Raises her eyebrows)* You want those?

KENNY. *(Shrugs)*… Here.

(KATE enters and sits at the other end of the lunchtable.)

LAUREN. *(taking the bag of carrots)* Did you notice that Daniel twists the twist ties ridiculously tight. They're carrots. They're not going anywhere. *(Maniacally twisting the twist tie with each word.)* You. Will. Like. Me. *(Crunches on a carrot)* There are 6 extra lunch monitors now.

KENNY. Because of what?

LAUREN. No. Since, you know, today. It's not that bad considering…

KENNY. It's pretty bad.

LAUREN. Yeah, /I know.

KENNY. You don't have to sit here.

LAUREN. Whatever.

(KENNY doesn't look at her, keeps drawing.)

LAUREN. Where's the drawing of me with the wings sitting on top of the cave? *(beat)* Why can't you draw a harp seal. *(beat)* I bet if you drew everyone their very own harp seal they'd chill out. Because harp seals are fuckin cute.

(KENNY ignores her and keeps drawing, doesn't look up.)

LAUREN. So. If you were going to shoot one person today, who would it be?

KENNY. No one./ No one. Be quiet.

LAUREN. One person. Fine, you don't have to shoot them, they would explode/ or catch fire.

KENNY. People don't just/explode.

LAUREN. It's a game Kenny. It's… okay, if you could explode someone due to natural/ causes.

KENNY. Don't touch me.

LAUREN. You need to explode someone before the end of lunch. Who's it gonna be?

KENNY. You.

LAUREN. Fine. I pick that kid with the guitar and the floppy hair.

KENNY. That kid? That's the nicest kid in school. He might be the only nice kid in school.

LAUREN. Well, I pick him, okay?

KENNY. Why?

LAUREN. He's not that nice.

KENNY. Neither are you.

LAUREN. I am too.

KENNY. This is a stupid game, it's not even/ fun…

LAUREN. *(To* KATE. *Loudly. Meanly.)* I'M SORRY. DO YOU NEED SOMETHING?

(A pause. KENNY *tenses up and looks offstage in the other direction.* KATE *gets up and exits.)*

KENNY. *(Looks at* **LAUREN***. Incredulous.)* What the hell/ was that?

LAUREN. What? That girl was staring at me.

KENNY. She wasn't staring at/ you.

LAUREN. Is this better than before? Everyone watching you and staying away?

KENNY. Yeah. I guess.

(*A pause.* **LAUREN** *looks around. This sucks.*)

LAUREN. You going to Gym?

KENNY. No. Counselor.

LAUREN. Mr. Goldberger's a douche.

KENNY. He's not that bad/.

LAUREN. "Well. Good morning young miss!"/ Young miss?

KENNY. Yeah, he's bad.

LAUREN. You don't have to tell him anything if you don't feel like it. Seriously, he's not a doctor. He used to sell insurance.

KENNY. Whatever.

LAUREN. Well what are you going to say if he asks why you didn't do it?

KENNY. Uh. I guess I'd tell him I didn't know if I'd be able to shoot myself afterwards.

LAUREN. …What?

KENNY. Because that's what you have to do… You go in there and then, you know, you/ have to…

LAUREN. *(upset by this)* Shut up. You do not.

KENNY. Yeah. That's the whole idea *(beat)*… What?

LAUREN. *(Really hurt)* You would have… You were going to leave me alone? I'd have to spend the rest of my life alone with Mom and Daniel? God…

KENNY. Well, I didn't.

LAUREN. … You're such an asshole.

KENNY. Hey. *(beat) Hey. (beat)* I'm right here. Eating chips.

(*He holds out the bag. She steals one of his chips. Bell rings. Lights fade on the lunchroom as lights rise on*)

THE COUNSELOR'S OFFICE

(**MR. GOLDBERGER** *sits at a desk.* **KENNY** *walks in holding his backpack. He's on the phone.*)

MR. GOLDBERGER. Sure, sure, in a few minutes, that'd be great. *(covering the phone)* Hello Mr. Barrett. You wanna drop that bag right over here?

(**KENNY** *looks at him. Puts his bag over by* **GOLDBERGER.** *Who opens it up, looks through it while he talks.*)

MR. GOLDBERGER. *(Laughs)* Thanks Annie. *(Hangs up the phone)* Well. Looks like you're doing okay./ You doing okay?

KENNY. Yeah. I'm fine. *(A quick pause)* Thank you for asking.

MR. GOLDBERGER. Oh sure. Everything go alright this morning with the, ah, was everything...

KENNY. *(Nodding).* Yeah, they were cool. Official/.

MR. GOLDBERGER. Not an easy way to start/ your day.

KENNY. It's fine.

MR. GOLDBERGER. They're only doing their job so don't take anything too personally. They're not out to, ah, it's the usual serve and protect and search, alright?

KENNY. Right. Sure./ It's fine.

MR. GOLDBERGER. Anything been difficult so far that you want to talk about? You had trouble with anyone?

KENNY. Nope.

MR. GOLDBERGER. How about that. Then that's the best thing I've heard so far today. Alright. *(pause)* So. Have you thought about what you're going to say?

KENNY. Yeah. *(beat)* Yeah. I wrote some stuff down, do you want me to... read it? It's... can I have my/ bag. It's in the...

MR. GOLDBERGER. Oh. Sure. *(handing him the bag)* Great that you got in there and took the initiative.

(KENNY digs out a piece of paper. MR. GOLDBERGER takes his bag back from him. KENNY looks at the paper. Reads.)

KENNY. People fuck up. Because things get so fucked up. People are assholes. People are untrustworthy. I know you all don't trust me. But, I guess what I can say is you don't have to trust me to feel safe. I can't use my car. I can't leave my house after school without an adult. I can't carry my coat around during the day. I can't walk through the hall without a monitor following me. I can't go online or buy anything or use my cell phone. Someone's watching me and my stuff all the time. So you only have to trust the people that are watching me. And they do a good job. We don't have to try to be friends now, we can't anyway. You don't have to talk to me. You don't have to look at me. Just let me be here for one more year. And don't be nervous.

(KENNY puts down his paper. Done.)

MR. GOLDBERGER. Kenny. You do realize you were supposed to write an apology.

KENNY. Yeah. That was it

MR. GOLDBERGER. I think you might need a "sorry" in there, my friend. Let's remember your audience. The entire school. Parents. School board members. C'mon. Let's jump right in and revise!

KENNY. I'm not sure/ I can…

MR. GOLDBERGER. Hey. Nothing to lose in here.

KENNY. Yeah… *(Pause)* I don't know what else to start with/… so

MR. GOLDBERGER. Well… *(pause)* Here. Jot down some notes. Freestyle. Whatever hits you. *(pause)*

KENNY. I should… Now?

MR. GOLDBERGER. I know, brainstorming is tough. Stick with me. I'm sorry…

KENNY. That you're all freaked out.

MR. GOLDBERGER. Yes, they're all freaked out but… what

are you sorry for. Yeah? I'm sorry that I...

KENNY. Got angry?

MR. GOLDBERGER. There! *(Pause. **KENNY** writes it down.)* You see that!...

KENNY. Yeah.

MR. GOLDBERGER. Well done, sir.

(A pause)

MR. GOLDBERGER. Are you still angry?

KENNY. ...No...

MR. GOLDBERGER. Maybe it'll help your classmates to hear that?

*(**KATE** walks into Mr. Goldberger's office.)*

KATE. Hi. Am I late?...

MR. GOLDBERGER. Hey. No! Come on in! Kenny, Kate. Kate, Kenny.

KATE. *(Looks at **KENNY**)* Hey.

KENNY. Hey. *(Standing, gathering up his stuff.)* So I'll/ get my...

MR. GOLDBERGER. Kate's going to join us. Sit. *(beat)* Sit. *(**KENNY** sits back down. **KATE** sits next to him.)* Hey. How's the new AP Physics guy? *(Begins looking through some folders.)*

KATE. Mr. Platt? Good. He's really good, actually. We're just reviewing vectors right now. Which is a little boring. But, yeah./He's great.

MR. GOLDBERGER. Shoot, I'm gonna go grab a few forms from the office. That okay with you. Kate?/ Do you feel comfortable waiting/ with...

KATE. Yeah sure.

MR. GOLDBERGER. Door open./ Right back.

KATE. It's fine. Thank you.

*(**GOLDBERGER** leaves. **KATE** and **KENNY** sit at the small round table. A pause.)*

KATE. Sorry, I didn't mean to interrupt your writing.

KENNY. Oh, no it's... not really writing.

KATE. Does it have to be a certain length?

KENNY. No. It has to be, better, I guess.

KATE. I can proofread it if you want. I have this weird radar for comma mistakes. They're the first thing my brain sees.

KENNY. That's cool.

KATE. Have you ever given a speech before?

KENNY. ...No.

KATE. It's not that bad. Whenever I speak in front of a large group, I try to visualize myself having gotten through the whole thing perfectly. Like when I presented my petition about cameras at the assembly to the school board.

KENNY. What cameras?

KATE. A bunch of the local tv stations and some morning show wanted to send cameras next week to tape your speech for the news.

KENNY. *(Pause. Totally freaked out.)* Can they do that?

KATE. They have to get permission for that kind of access. Otherwise, they're stuck standing across the street speculating on what's going on inside with a shot of the school in the background.

KENNY. Oh.

KATE. So I got 500 community signatures and presented my case at the last school board meeting. And now, no cameras.

KENNY. Why?

KATE. Uh. Because the petition worked.

KENNY. *(beat)* Yeah, no, I meant why did you petition?

KATE. Oh... I don't know. I figured... Someone should do something to help... *(beat)* I mean, you were in my English class last year so...

KENNY. Yeah...

KATE. And I was born to organize people so petitions are my bread and butter.

KENNY. I don't know. *(A pause)* Are you in band?

KATE. No. Why?

KENNY. Uhm… It's…

(She looks at him. **KENNY** *shrugs. A pause.* **GOLD-BERGER** *reenters.)*

MR. GOLDBERGER. Alright! *(Waving some papers)* Now. Kenny. This young lady is one of our best. You know anything about each other? *(***KENNY** *shakes his head)* Kate's a National Merit Scholar, vice president of Model UN right?. And she won the Prudential Spirit of the Community Award last year for (don't roll your eyes, young miss, it's very prestigious, you should be proud) working to donate 600 prom dresses to needy girls who want to go to, uh, prom.

KENNY. Oh. *(No idea how to respond to this resume. Looks at* **KATE.***)*

MR. GOLDBERGER. And now, Kate's volunteered to be your student mentor.

KENNY. For what?

MR. GOLDBERGER. We do it all the time for new students. Someone just hangs with you, shows you around, sits with you during free periods. To/ help you ease back in.

KATE. To ease you back in. Officially.

KENNY. …Yeah.

MR. GOLDBERGER. You think it through. Take these forms home, have your mom look it over.

KATE. And I can come by your house and meet her if she wants.

MR. GOLDBERGER. That's a great idea.

KATE. She can make sure I'm up to snuff. *(***KENNY** *doesn't respond. Embarassed.)* So, I'm gonna sign it now and then go/ back to…

MR. GOLDBERGER. Oh. Sure sure. Vectors.

KATE. Vectors wait for no one.

*(***KATE** *does. Signs it. Hands it to* **KENNY.** *Who looks at her. She exits.* **MR. GOLDBERGER** *looks at him.)*

KENNY. But... I've gone here for three years.

MR. GOLDBERGER. But this. Is a new beginning.

*(He looks at **KENNY**. **KENNY** looks at him signs the paper. Then, he picks up his pen and begins writing.)*

KENNY. I've gone here for three years but this... is a new beginning.

*(**GOLDBERGER** smiles tightly, hands **KENNY** another piece of paper. Lights out as lights rise on*

THE PARKING LOT

(LAUREN standing outside, her jacket on. KENNY stands next to her, his backpack on the ground next to his saxophone case.)

LAUREN. She forgot. It's such a drag they won't let you drive anymore. You got me everywhere on time. I can't believe/ she forgot.

KENNY. Call her again.

LAUREN. I told her not to sign me up for the 4:00 class. I don't even like ballet.

KENNY. Then why do you go?

LAUREN. Whatever. I don't hate it. Okay? It's better than going straight home.

KENNY. Thanks.

LAUREN. Well, it is. *(beat, looking offstage left.)* What's up with him? He stands there looking pissed off until you leave school grounds.

KENNY. Pretty much. He has to make sure an adult is in the car and Mom has to sign me out.

LAUREN. Dude. They can pay me to do that. I watch The Wire. God! It's not like she's a surgeon!

KENNY. What are you/ talking about?

LAUREN. I'm saying, she could justify being late all the time if she were stuck doing a triple bypass. But she's setting up some new display at a department store and probably got wrapped up "visually merchandising" a bunch of/ lamps so people will buy them faster.

KENNY. Okay. I get it.

LAUREN. She forgot.

KENNY. She'll be here.

LAUREN. Shit.

KENNY. What?

LAUREN. Look the other... don't look at him.

(CHARLIE walks onstage, tuning his guitar with harmonica attachment strapped to his chest like armor. He starts to tune. LAUREN ignores him. KENNY stares.)

CHARLIE. Hey man. How you doin?

(**CHARLIE** *returns to tuning.* **LAUREN** *is mortified.* **CHARLIE**, *done tuning strums a big open chord and begins.*)

CHARLIE. *(singing)*

If we lived by the ocean, I would take you to the ocean

But we don't so I can't but if we were there

We would stand on the sand and I'd hand you my sunglasses

So you could see the ocean without squinting through the glare.

And baby, ahhhh,

Maybe we would stand there forever.

I can't see but who cares if we're together.

Cause baby, ahhh... maybe

(**CHARLIE** *stops. He looks at* **KENNY**.)

CHARLIE. Can you take that part?

KENNY. ...No...

CHARLIE. It's just that one... I'll sing "And baby", then you come right in with Ahhhhhh. So it's like, *(singing)* And baby, Ahhhhhhh. Just watch me for it. *(Hits the guitar, 2,3,4)*

CHARLIE. *(singing)*

And baby, *(cues* **KENNY** *with a big nod)*

(**KENNY**: *Ah.*)

Maybe we would stand there forever.

I can't see but I know we're together.

'Cause baby *(cues* **KENNY** *who misses it)* when it's you and me

There's nowhere else I want to be

On the drive home from the beach we would buy something lame

At a souvenir shop like a personalized mini license plate.

We could play one of those stupid car games
Like I spy with my blue eye a girl I think is great.

And baby, *(KENNY: Ahh)*
Maybe we would drive on forever.
I don't know how but we'd do it together.
'Cause baby *(KENNY: Ahh)* when it's you and me.
There's nowhere else I want to be

(KENNY unsure of what to do, stares at LAUREN. LAUREN looks at him.)

CHARLIE. Yeah, I'm still working on the chorus so it's not quite finished but...

LAUREN. Do you ever stop talking?

CHARLIE. Yes. And you know, I wrote you that song. I wrote it because when I see you, normally, it's just, it's just a mess. When I think about you I can't breathe and I look at you and I'm not sure you're real. You just look like... Like if someone were to say, Hey can you draw a girl and I drew you they'd be like, hey, that's a perfect drawing of a girl, you're a real good artist. And my hands get all shaky when I want to touch you and you know that great hollow feeling you get in your stomach when you see someone you've been thinking about for days and then you turn the corner and there they are. And it's like... *(he exhales all the air in his lungs until the breath just stops)* And the bottom drops out and I feel like I have no actual mass or dimension and it's like maybe I'm seeing you at that moment after having thought about you because you were, at the same time, thinking about me. And that's how we ended up at the exact same place in the exact same moment. By thinking about it that much. Do you need a ride?

LAUREN. I thought you take the bus.

CHARLIE. Well, no. I took the bus because I drove by and saw you. So I parked and walked back to the stop. Then I went back and got the car. So, basically, I/ drove and took the...

LAUREN. *(interrupting)* Yeah. I need a ride to my dance class.

CHARLIE. Great. You going with her?

KENNY. I can't, uh, you can't just give me a ride.

LAUREN. My mom's on her way.

CHARLIE. We can wait with you.

KENNY/LAUREN. No.

CHARLIE. *(to* LAUREN*).* So. /There's a dance on Friday…

LAUREN. Do you want me to call her again?

KENNY. No.

CHARLIE. Are you going? Has anyone asked you?

LAUREN. What? No. I don't dance.

CHARLIE. Oh. And yet, I'm driving you to dance class.

LAUREN. I don't go. To dances. It's not my thing. *(beat)* What?

CHARLIE. No. Nothing.

LAUREN. Cool. *(To* KENNY*)* So I'm/ gonna..

CHARLIE. Will you go to the dance with me? *(strums a chord)* Take a chance on me? *(chord)* Find romance with me? *(chord, he sings)* In the big, blue cafeteria of my soul. *(He begins to strum repeatedly about to launch into another song).* /And I will…

LAUREN. Fine. Fine! Shut up! I'll go! *(beat)* I'll only go if Kenny can come with us.

CHARLIE. Yeah. *(beat)* Of course. *(beat)* Like a group thing? Like a brother chaperone type thing?

LAUREN. He'll have a date.

CHARLIE. Rock on. Who's your date?

KENNY. I'm not going.

CHARLIE. Kenny. I'd really like it if you came with us. You play that horn? Man, we can hang out while Lauren gets dressed and jam.

KENNY. It was a gift/. I don't…

CHARLIE. We'll only stay as long as you want. Please. Right now I want you to go to this dance with me more than anyone else in the whole school.

*(*LAUREN*'s cell phone rings)*

LAUREN. *(Into the phone)* Hey. We're fine. Mom. He's fine. No, I got a ride to class so... Yeah, a ride. Yes in a car. We're fine Mom. *(to* **KENNY***)* She's on her way.

*(***LAUREN*** ends the call. She and ***CHARLIE*** exit. ***KENNY*** stands there waiting puts his bag on his shoulder. Lights shift around him and we are now at)*

THE CAMPGROUNDS

(GRACE enters stage left holding a casserole dish covered with tin foil. Stage right, half an unmade tent appears on the ground. GRACE and KENNY look offstage right where CAROLINE is unseen, staking the other side of the tent.)

GRACE. I don't understand why you won't stay at our house.

(The tent now assembled, CAROLINE enters from offstage.)

CAROLINE. I like this. Is that… a lasagna?

GRACE. Daniel made it so we thought we'd bring it by and have dinner with you. Al fresco.

CAROLINE. *(Takes it from GRACE)* Oh. Awesome. *(She puts it down)* How was school?

KENNY. It was okay.

GRACE. Here, you hold, I'll serve. *(She hands KENNY the plates)*

CAROLINE. Sure. *(to KENNY)* Yeah? What'd happened?

KENNY. Uh, you know, I went to class, talked to the counselor, stuff like that.

GRACE. Tell her about band!

KENNY. I went to band. I watched. They played.

CAROLINE. I didn't know you were in band?

GRACE. He/started playing the saxophone! You know your grandfather heard John Coltrane play twice.

KENNY. *(To CAROLINE)* I'm not really. *(To GRACE)* Yeah, I know.

CAROLINE. Do you have forks?

GRACE. Of course. *(Pulls cloth napkins, rolled up complete with napkin holders from her bag.)*

CAROLINE. Cloth napkins?

GRACE. What?

CAROLINE. No! It's nice. Hey, do you guys want to sit…
(looking around)

GRACE. Do you have chairs?

CAROLINE. No. But *(enlisting* **KENNY***)* see that couple over there.

KENNY. The ones making out against the tree?

CAROLINE. That's Josh and Jennifer, they're on their honeymoon.

GRACE. Oh. Don't bother them if/ they're on their honeymoon.

CAROLINE. They've got all this extra gear. Trade them. Lasagna for chairs. *(Picks up the casserole dish hand it to* **KENNY***)*

KENNY. Okay.

*(***KENNY*** exits with the casserole dish. They watch him go.)*

CAROLINE. He seems alright.

GRACE. Well. He's lucky.

CAROLINE. He's lucky, we're lucky. It could have /been…

GRACE. Does it look like he's limping?

CAROLINE. A little. You can hardly notice.

GRACE. I had to give away his horrible dogs today.

CAROLINE. You gave/his…

GRACE. Yes. Because they attacked him this morning.

CAROLINE. Well, then that sounds like the right move.

GRACE. And they kept looking at me like *(hangdog look)*, like they knew exactly what I was going to do. It was so depressing and I don't even like animals.

CAROLINE. How'd he take it?

GRACE. When we went home and he saw they were gone I told him they were at the groomers.

CAROLINE. Grace!

GRACE. What was I supposed to say?! I gave them to a no kill shelter.

CAROLINE. I wouldn't lead with that. *(sneaks a taste of lasagna)* Wow…

GRACE. I know.

CAROLINE. He cooks?

GRACE. Almost every night. We were going to have a big dinner at home but, Kenny wanted to come over here and see you so I thought this would be a good distraction… *(sniffs)* Is someone smoking pot.

CAROLINE. Oh I was like an hour ago. You can still smell it?

GRACE. Are you stoned?

CAROLINE. Barely… I unpacked, I smoked a bowl, I took a walk. *(beat)* What?

GRACE. Nothing. *(beat)* Really! It's… sometimes, I still can't believe you've actually made a career out of wandering around wherever you want, digging roads, building huts, smoking pot and sending off weird beaded tunics for Christmas. *(beat)* No, I mean, good for you. Truly. No one thought it'd work out. Entirely to your credit.

CAROLINE. I thought you liked the tunics.

GRACE. I do. I kept all of them. I can show them to you.

CAROLINE. I know what they look like.

GRACE. So. Is this your usual 48 hours every two or three years?

CAROLINE. *(beat, then brightly)* You know me!

> (**KENNY** *walks back over carrying two lawn chairs and a lantern. He opens up the chairs and sets them on either side of* **CAROLINE** *who sits on the ground)*

KENNY. They made me take this too.

GRACE. That's so thoughtful. (**GRACE** *sits.* **CAROLINE** *gives them a wave. They sit and eat.)*

CAROLINE. Hey! A toast! *(holds up her water bottle)* To your first day and to one more exciting new arrival.

GRACE. Why? Who else is coming?

CAROLINE. Hey, Look me in the eye when you cheers. Otherwise it's bad luck. You know… Everyone getting ready for another baby… ?

KENNY. *(Looking her in the eye as they bump water bottles)* What baby? *(beat.* **GRACE** *realizes.)*

CAROLINE. Oh. God, I didn't... /I thought...

GRACE. No. It's fine. *(To Kenny)* There's no baby. Daniel wants to have baby and apparently he's been talking about it. I should have said something and that's my fault. *(beat)* Also. Your dogs aren't at the groomers, I had to give them away because of the biting. I'm / sorry but...

KENNY. What?

GRACE. Your leg could have been your face. Or someone elses face./ You can't control them...

KENNY. They're not yours. You can't get rid of dogs that aren't yours.

GRACE. I didn't put them to sleep.

KENNY. You were going to put them to sleep?

GRACE. NO! I gave them to a no kill shelter so they won't... do that./ They get to run around all day.

KENNY. What if I do everything everybody says? Then can they come back?

GRACE. Sweetie, even if they aren't horrible attack dogs, they look like they might become that/ at some point.

KENNY. They're not attack dogs. Can someone we know take them for a while instead?

GRACE. We'll see. *(pause)* Hey. We'll see.

KENNY. *(Almost to himself)* Yeah. Or maybe I'll take away something of yours.

GRACE. Well, you've... *(Stops herself)*

CAROLINE. So you're not /pregnant?

GRACE. What? No.

CAROLINE. You're not too old, are you?

GRACE. No, it's not that I'm, Jesus Christ, how can you ask that?/Who actually asks someone that...

CAROLINE. I didn't mean, not that biologically you couldn't make it happen, just are you past the point emotionally where/ you'd want to go through...

GRACE. I'm sure if I... what's that smell?

KENNY. Fire. That guy Josh is making a fire. *(beat)* You'd be 61. When the/ baby turns 20, you'd be 61.

GRACE. Okay. Thank you. Enough.

(A pause. They eat.)

GRACE. It's so quiet. *(pause)*

CAROLINE. You should go camping here sometime.

KENNY. We've never been camping.

GRACE. Yes you have. Remember when you were seven and you and your sister wanted to go camping and your father set up the tent in the backyard?

KENNY. Yeah.

GRACE. So. What do you call that?

KENNY. Sleeping in a tent in the backyard.

KENNY. Can I stay here tonight?

GRACE. No, it's a school night.

KENNY. But I could. Right? She's an adult.

GRACE. Technically, yes, she is.

CAROLINE. Another time, okay? *(To KENNY)* Hey! You want to learn how to make a fire? Wilderness-style. No matches.

GRACE. No. Sorry, it's getting late.

CAROLINE. C'mon. We can make a bonfire.

GRACE. *(Folding up her chair)* Thanks, but we should go. Kenny, can you take these chairs back/ to those nice people.

KENNY. Whatever. They said they don't care/ about…

GRACE. Please take the chairs back. Now.

(KENNY gathers up the chairs. Exits)

GRACE. *(Irritated)* Without matches? Really?

CAROLINE. Some people discover huge reserves of self confidence when they're mastering a new skill.

GRACE. I KNOW! That's why I got him the saxophone!

CAROLINE. What, you think he's going to burn the house down while you sleep?

GRACE. Well at least then I wouldn't have to sell it.

CAROLINE. You're selling the hou/se?

GRACE. Yes, Not trying to have a baby. Trying to sell the house. Anything else?

CAROLINE. But… You love that house. It's the house where everything happens. Christmas. Thanksgiving. The other ones.

GRACE. You don't come home for holidays anymore.

CAROLINE. I know. But I kinda think of your house as my house. Even though I never lived there.

GRACE. Well now it's "that kid's house"/ so I don't think…

CAROLINE. That'll go away.

GRACE. No it won't.

(Beat. They both look over toward the newlywed camping couple.)

CAROLINE. What's he doing over there?

GRACE. He's roasting marshmallows with strangers.

CAROLINE. That's sweet.

GRACE. He doesn't want to leave yet.

CAROLINE. Yeah, who can resist S'mores.

GRACE. It's not that. He likes being around you.

(Beat.)

GRACE. It's good to be together again.

CAROLINE. Like a really bad party.

GRACE. It's funny, I always think it's going to be nicer than it actually is.*(beat)* That fire smells great doesn't it.

CAROLINE. We can go over. *(beat)* C'mon. Marshmallows…

GRACE. No, you go ahead. Just we need to leave soon so…

CAROLINE. Five minutes?

GRACE. Sure.

*(**CAROLINE** exits. **GRACE** watches them. Lights out and lights up on)*

THE KITCHEN

*(Friday morning. **KENNY** sits at the table looking at a fish in a bowl. **LAUREN** enters.)*

LAUREN. Are you gonna name it?

KENNY. I'll name it when it actually does something.

DANIEL. Hey, what do you want for lunch today?

KENNY. I don't/ care.

(Phone rings. Phone rings.)

LAUREN. Don't make me anything. I told you I'm making my own lunch now.

DANIEL. *(Throwing a loaf of bread onto the counter in prep)* Where's the cordless it's not in the thingie.

*(**GRACE** enters.)*

GRACE. Hey, how about a real breakfast for a change? You want some eggs?

KENNY. I'm not hungry.

*(**DANIEL** finds the phone holds it triumphantly over his head. **GRACE** goes to grab cereal bowls.)*

GRACE. Well, at least/ have some cereal.

DANIEL. Hello? Hey. *(Listening. Walking upstairs, exiting.)* No it's not too early. What's up.

GRACE. How are you feeling today?

KENNY. You ask me about how I feel too much.

GRACE. Okay. How do you feel?

LAUREN. Amazing. *(beat)* What's your deal? You have a date or not? The dance is tonight and we can't just go as three people, we'll look like idiots.

GRACE. A date! Sweetie that's… that's so ambitious!

LAUREN. He doesn't have one yet.

GRACE. I can go with you.

KENNY. No.

LAUREN. *(overlapping)* No you can't.

GRACE. He has to have an adult there regardless. And I'm a great dancer. Did you know my senior year/ I was the prom queen?

LAUREN. God! He doesn't want to actually go with you! Tell her!

KENNY. I'm not going.

GRACE. Oh! You can ask your mentor!

KENNY. No, /I don't…

GRACE. You must like her a little. And I can tell she likes you. She wouldn't be coming over here today to help you with your speech if she didn't/ like you.

KENNY. I miss my dogs. *(He drops some food in the bowl for the fish)* Here you go. I hate you.

GRACE. Don't say that. /That's a beta fish. They're very popular.

LAUREN. It can't hear him. It's not a real pet.

GRACE. Where's your bag?

LAUREN. Upstairs.

GRACE. Why don't you go get it. We're leaving in 5 minutes.

(LAUREN heads upstairs as DANIEL reenters holding a bunch of clothes for the dry cleaners, puts them on the chair. Moving to make the lunches, he looks at LAUREN moving past him.)

DANIEL. *(Chipper, to GRACE)* I've got the day off! The regional manager is coming to do some training so… *(To LAUREN)* Hey, if you've got clothes for the cleaners, bring em down, okay?

LAUREN. /Fine.

(As CAROLINE enters, DANIEL moves to the counter looks in Lauren's lunch bag and takes an apple and a soda out, disapprovingly. He begins to make sandwiches. KENNY begins practicing his knot tying.)

CAROLINE. Hey! Guys! Have you seen what's going on outside?

LAUREN. *(exiting upstairs)* No and I don't care. Seriously, I cannot be late again/ this week.

GRACE. Did you walk here?

CAROLINE. Yeah, your neighbor's yard is flooding, the gardeners hit a pipe.

GRACE. What? Oh! Your shoes are covered in mud. Just... stand right there please.

CAROLINE. I can fix it but they've gotta turn off the water right away.

GRACE. *(To DANIEL, exiting)* Oh my god. Is Bonnie even home?

DANIEL. You know how to fix pipes?

CAROLINE. Yes I do. Ooh! Can I help make lunches?

DANIEL. That's alright, I've got it. *(Sotto)* Can you just find out what he wants to eat.

CAROLINE. *(To KENNY)* Hey. Peanut Butter and Jelly?

KENNY. Fine. With crusts

CAROLINE. *(Proudly, to Daniel)* With crusts.

GRACE. It's a disaster. I need to call the water company before it floods our side yard. Where's the phone?

DANIEL. I left it in the bedroom.

GRACE. *(calling upstairs)* Lauren! Bring me the cordless / from our bedroom!

DANIEL. Do you need us to drive you to the airport tomorrow?

CAROLINE. Oh, I don't know yet but thanks.

GRACE. But you're leaving tomorrow.

CAROLINE. I might stay through the weekend.

(**LAUREN** *comes downstairs with the cordless, a shirt and her bag and takes one look at* **CAROLINE.** *Tosses her mom the phone and takes off.*)

LAUREN. I gotta go I'm taking the bus.

(*She exits.* **GRACE** *looks at* **CAROLINE.**)

GRACE. Just... don't... sit, don't move. Okay? I'll get you a towel.

(**GRACE** *moves out of the room to make her call and get a towel.*)

CAROLINE. Oh! Dude! I have something for you. *(She opens her bag and pulls out a coil of rope).*

You need more than that little scrap of rope to really practice. C'mon. I'll time you. *(beat)* Really. Tie me to this chair with a double figure 8. Go. GO!

*(**KENNY** looks at **DANIEL** who nods his permission. He begins.)*

KENNY. Mom said she was the prom queen once. Were you?

CAROLINE. No. Why?

KENNY. I don't know. There's a dance. I can't go with my Mom.

CAROLINE. No. God, who suggested that?

KENNY. She did. She sounded sort of... excited. But... I never... asked her to go. How do I get her not to go if I never...

CAROLINE. Just get another date. Someone who didn't give birth to you.

KENNY. I'm done. *(beat)* Wait, no. *(Pulls the rope more securely around **CAROLINE**)* I'm done.

CAROLINE. Not bad. *(beat)* Look. All you have to do is walk up to a girl and boom! ask her straight up, hey, do you want to go to the dance. Not complicated but you should smile. And maybe add a personal detail.

KENNY. That won't work.

CAROLINE. It will. Trust me. Just ask and then talk about something else. Your toes. The weather. Anything.

KENNY. Will you go?*(A pause. Smiles)* My toes are shorter than most peoples toes, My toes are short for my feet but I like them. *(Beat)* How was that?

CAROLINE. With me?

KENNY. Yeah.

*(A pause. **KENNY** embarrassed.)*

KENNY. Nevermind.

DANIEL. Hey, go get the rest of your stuff. I've gotta go through your bag.

(**KENNY** *gestures to the knapsack at* **DANIEL**'s *feet.*
DANIEL *starts to go through* **KENNY**'s *bag. Before* **KENNY**
can take off...)

CAROLINE. How are you getting there? I don't have a car.
Or a valid license. *(To* **DANIEL***)* Are you taking him?

KENNY. We can go with Lauren's friend Charlie. He has a
car. 6:00.

CAROLINE. I'll be here.

(**KENNY** *exits upstairs with the fishbowl.* **DANIEL** *looks
at* **CAROLINE** *and laughs.*)

CAROLINE. What? He asked. It's better than going with his
actual mom. And besides, I'll get to be there for him.
Since I'm never here, I don't get to... show up/...
much.

DANIEL. You're right, no, you're right. I... I should have
offered to be there as his... his fade into the background adult or... I don't know... *(beat)* I wish he
wanted me to go. That's weird isn't it.

CAROLINE. No. It's not. It's selfish. But it's sweet.

DANIEL. What does that mean?

CAROLINE. I mean, they don't like you. And that must be
really hard.

DANIEL. Well they're teenagers. They don't like anything,
right?

CAROLINE. Sure.

DANIEL. So, what, you think it's wrong that I want to have a
kid who likes me?

CAROLINE. No I don't, /I think...

DANIEL. I don't blame him, okay? Would you like me if I
had to search everything you owned. *(zips up the bag)*
God, I feel awful. Look at this, I'm sweating.

CAROLINE. Do you need some Advil?/ Or...

DANIEL. I, I want to go to movie. I want to sit in a movie
theater all afternoon.

CAROLINE. So go. *(beat)* Disappear for a few hours! Go to
a movie!

DANIEL. Yeah. I'm not sure that's what I should be doing.

CAROLINE. Isn't that why it'd make you feel better.

(KENNY enters carrying the form. DANIEL signs it.)

KENNY. You taking me? To school?

DANIEL. Yeah. Hey. You want to pull the car out of the garage?

KENNY. No, it's okay. *(beat)* Thanks.

(KENNY exits. GRACE walks back into the room on the cordless.)

GRACE. *(entering)* Yes it's 2645 Vine. I'll be over to let him in.

DANIEL. Hey! Hey Gracie. Let's take the day off.

CAROLINE. Yeah! C'mon!

DANIEL. We can go to a movie!

GRACE. During the day? I thought you were /going to go...

DANIEL. No. I am. Kenny. Car Wash. Grocery store. Dry Cleaning./ I am.

GRACE. Ugh. This kitchen is a mess. Where's Kenny.

(She begins straightening up.)

DANIEL. In the car, I'm taking him in a minute. I mean when I get back. All of us.

CAROLINE. We can go to the mall!

DANIEL. We can steal something!

CAROLINE. No. I don't steal. We're not stealing anything.

DANIEL. Right, no, that's/ not fun.

CAROLINE. Did you steal things?

DANIEL. I went through a phase./ When I was in college after my mom died.

GRACE. You went through /a what?

CAROLINE. Hey, can we get some beer?

GRACE. No.

CAROLINE. Fine,/ god...

GRACE. We're not all on vacation.

CAROLINE. I heard you. Jesus… .

GRACE. I'm already late and now I have to let the some guy from the water company into Bonnie's basement since we have her emergency keys. *(beat)* So, are you/ going to…

DANIEL. Yes. Kenny. Car Wash. Grocery.

(He starts to exit. She holds out the lunch and an armful of drycleaning)

GRACE. Dry cleaning.

DANIEL. *(beat)* Dry cleaning.

(He takes the lunch and clothes, exits. **GRACE** *looks after him.)*

CAROLINE. Does he seem sad?

GRACE. No. Why? Did he say something?

CAROLINE. No. *(beat)* Hey, I can clean up in here.

GRACE. Oh you don't have to do that.

CAROLINE. I know. I'd just/ like to.

GRACE. It's fine, I'm finished. *(Moving to leave. Turns around, starting.)* Caroline… You *(looking at her closely)* You still have little dirt splatters everywhere. All over your…

CAROLINE. I do?

GRACE. So you're staying through the weekend?

CAROLINE. I think so.

GRACE. *(Pulls a bit of mud out of her hair)* See? Mud. Why don't you go upstairs and shower. You can borrow something clean. If you want.

(**GRACE** *exits leaving* **CAROLINE** *in the kitchen covered in mud. Lights out.)*

THE KITCHEN

(The kitchen, after school. **KATE** *and* **KENNY** *are standing on chairs facing each other.* **KENNY** *is holding a xeroxed piece of paper.)*

KATE. The most important thing, besides speaking clearly is making sure you look up and out on all the highlighted words. To connect with your audience.

KENNY. On all of them?

KATE. Looking up is almost more important than what you're saying.

KENNY. *(Looking at the paper)* Uh. This isn't my speech.

KATE. *(Laughing)* I know! Yeah, I figured it'd be easier to practice these techniques if we used a different speech.

KENNY. Oh. Okay.

KATE. And remember, you'll be standing on a stage and it's going to feel weird but when you look up, you have to look up and out. Shoulders back. *(Looking at him)* Oh. You're probably going to have to cut your bangs. *(He pushes his hair out of his face a little.)* Better.

*(**KATE** gets down off her chair and sits in it like an audience member. **KENNY** still stands on his chair, shoulders back and starts plowing through the speech.)*

KENNY. Good afternoon as anyone close to me knows for months I have been grappling with how best to reconcile myself to the American people to acknowledge my own wrongdoing and still to maintain my focus on the work of the presidency.

KATE. Okay! That's great! But lift your chin and aim your eyes at the back wall when you look up.

KENNY. Who wrote this?

KATE. President Clinton.

KENNY. It's pretty good.

KATE. Yeah. One more thing. You have to respect the commas. Everytime you see a comma, take a little breath in. Okay?

KENNY. What I want the American people to know *(takes a breath)* what I want the Congress to know *(takes a breath)* is that I am profoundly sorry for all I have done wrong in words and deeds. *(Losing his place)* Uh. Oh. Quite simply I gave into my shame. And while it's hard for you to hear yourself called deceitful and manipulative, I remember Ben Franklin's admonition that our critics are our friends for they do show us our faults.

KATE. Not bad! But try to breathe more quietly.

KENNY. Yeah.

KATE. Really take that pause before your last important point. It's like a silent drumroll. And your shoulders keep going up when you talk... Keep reminding yourself back and down.

KENNY. Okay.

KATE. There you go. I'm sorry. Is this too much?

KENNY. No. It's okay. *(beat)* Back. And Down.

(GRACE enters.)

GRACE. Are you two sure you don't want a snack?

KATE. Oh, I'm fine./ We're almost done.

KENNY. We're fine. *(Getting off the chair.)*

GRACE. Something to drink? We have Coke, orange-mango-pineapple juice, seltzer, diet sprite, milk, water.

KATE. Oh I'll definitely have some milk.

GRACE. Okay. Two big glasses of milk coming up.

KENNY. I don't want any.

GRACE. I do. A big cold glass of milk sounds good to me, too.

KATE. Yeah, I don't drink any soda at all.

GRACE. Really!

KATE. Yeah, my parents never had it in the house so I never even think about it.

GRACE. That's so interesting. All Kenny's sister wanted when she was a baby was soda. Sometimes the only thing that could get her to stop crying was if she saw me pouring Dr. Pepper in her bottle.

KATE. *(Unsure)...* Wow

GRACE. I thought it was the fizzing sound that soothed her. She would suck down a bottle of Dr. Pepper and then take a nap. *(beat)* Well I don't want to hold you up, I'm sure you're anxious to get home and start getting ready for that dance tonight.

KATE. Oh. Yeah.

GRACE. Are you/ going?

KENNY. Can I have some milk?

GRACE. Of course. *(Gets up and pours him a glass.)*

KATE. One last thing. I'd type out your speech in big font and then paste it on notecards.

GRACE. Those are good tips. Aren't they? And I want to tell you, I think it's very brave of you to come over here/ and help Kenny.

KATE. Oh, it's nothing.

GRACE. No, it is. It's not something a lot of other kids would do. Put themselves out there like this for one of their classmates.

KATE. I like doing this. Volunteering.

GRACE. We're all so glad you and Kenny are becoming friends.

KATE. Yeah.

GRACE. And Kenny is too.

KENNY. Uh. I'll be right/ back I have to...

(KENNY *exits, upstairs*)

GRACE. He's nervous. I'm sure you've noticed he gets nervous around you. It's sweet, don't you think.,

(LAUREN *enters, carrying her backpack*)

KATE. *(Embarassed)* Oh. Sure.

GRACE. *(Happily)* Lauren!

LAUREN. *(beat.)* Yeah.

GRACE. Do you know Kate?

LAUREN. No.

KATE. Hey. I'm Kate. I'm in your gym class.

LAUREN. Oh. Right. Hi.

KATE. Hi.

GRACE. Where were you?

LAUREN. I had to retake a quiz.

GRACE. How'd it go?

LAUREN. It sucked. Are you drinking milk together?

GRACE. We are! Would you like some?

LAUREN. No.

GRACE. How is it you two don't know each other?

KATE. We're not in the same grade. But I know Lauren. I mean, I know who she is.

LAUREN. Yeah. You know what other people say about me so that basically means you know me. Right?

KATE. I guess…

LAUREN. You hang out in the English department offices all the time, don't you? The teachers in there totally love you.

KATE. Yeah, they're great.

LAUREN. Mrs. Gordon was talking about you today. About how my brother's helping you write something?

KATE. Oh. No. I'm helping him work on his speech for the assembly on Monday.

LAUREN. Sorry, I must have gotten it wrong. I thought he was helping you. *(Pause)* Are you going to the dance?

KATE. I guess so.

LAUREN. Do you have a date?

KATE. Not really, a few of/ us are…

LAUREN. Why don't you ask my brother to go?

GRACE. I think that's between Kate/ and Kenny…

KATE. I didn't think he'd/ want to go…

GRACE. Of course he'd want to go with you!

LAUREN. I mean, as his official ambassador, don't you think it's your responsibility? To help him have a good time?

KATE. That's not really what the mentor program is about. I think going on dates with the person you're mentoring is discouraged, actually…

LAUREN. Seriously? That's strange because you ask everyone questions about him, you stare at him all the time.
And now you're over at our house. It looks like you
really want on him.

GRACE. Lauren!

KATE. No! *(To* GRACE*)* It's not like that.

GRACE. What's wrong/ with you?

LAUREN. Why do you need to know everything about him?

KATE. We're getting to know each other.

LAUREN. Really. And you're not writing all this shit about
my brother for your college essay?

KATE. I'm not…

LAUREN. And you're going to lie about it to my face?

GRACE. Stop! She's not writing about him, she's helping
him/ with his…

KATE. No. I wrote about how it feels to come back to /
school after…

LAUREN. Bullshit. I heard this teacher talking about how
she was so moved by what you wrote about "the Barrett
boy". *(To* GRACE*)* They're going to publish it in all the
papers. Apparently it's very well written. Lots of detail.
Mrs. Gordon said it gets inside his head, makes you
realize just how disturbed he must have been. How
teachers still can't get other kids to sit near him or
work with him in class. You know how that medicine
gave him that tic under his left eye and if he can't get it
under control he gets so upset his hands start shaking.
She wrote about that because the school nurse fucking
TOLD HER and… I told him not to talk to anyone.
Why does everyone need to know about that? Why do
you have to write about my brother? Why don't you
write about something else.

KATE. It's… He's more compelling.

(KENNY *reenters.*)

LAUREN. Does he know you're writing down everything he
says while you/ help him with his speech.

KATE. I'm not. And even if I was, he doesn't talk that much
so it wouldn't really add all that much.

GRACE. *(Pause)* Did you know about this?

KENNY. What.

KATE. I'm helping him ease back into things.

GRACE. Which papers are going to publish your essay?

KATE. It's not necessarily going to/ run in… .

GRACE. Which ones.

KATE. The Tribune, The Pioneer Press and the Reader but it's not… a big deal. *(a beat)*

GRACE. Do you need a ride home?

KATE. *(beat)* Uh. No, I can walk from here.

> *(KATE picks up her backpack as LAUREN and KENNY stand there.)*

LAUREN. You know, I have a lot of really compelling problems. You could probably help me with them since you're so good at it. Maybe we can hang out sometime.

> *(KATE exits. LAUREN and KENNY look at each other.)*

KENNY. What happened/ to… ?

LAUREN. *(angrily)* You didn't do anything.

KENNY. What?

LAUREN. I saw you. *(beat)* You didn't even almost do it. You barely pointed it at anyone, you just waved it around all half assed. You almost dropped it right on your foot. Seriously, you can't hold on to anything.

KENNY. I didn't know/ you…

LAUREN. And it wasn't even loaded. You were terrible, actually.

> *(LAUREN exits as CAROLINE enters wearing a fancy blouse and skirt and a little makeup. She looks pretty.)*

CAROLINE. Can I wear a t-shirt with this skirt?

GRACE. What?

CAROLINE. I feel like a nurse in this blouse. I feel like a nurse who's trying too hard. No offense. It's pretty it's just not… me *(to KENNY)* Is that weird? If I wear a t-shirt to the dance?

GRACE. You're going to the dance?

CAROLINE. Daniel didn't tell you?

GRACE. No. I don't know where he is. He hasn't been home all day and he's not picking up his phone. So. No. He didn't tell me.

CAROLINE. Oh. I didn't/ know that he...

KENNY. She's an adult. That means I can go with her.

GRACE. Yes. You can. *(beat)* You have to sign him in and out, okay?

CAROLINE. Yeah. Definitely.

*(She exits to change her shirt. **KENNY** stands with **GRACE** in the kitchen. Tense and unsure of what to do.)*

GRACE. *(A beat)* It's great that you're going to the dance.

KENNY. ...yeah.

GRACE. And you can wear whatever you want.

KENNY. I know.

GRACE. If you like that, just wear that/. Alright? It looks fine.

KENNY. *(Nods)*... Yeah.

GRACE. And call when you want a ride home. If you want to leave early, I'll come get you. You can come home whenever you want.

KENNY. Okay.

GRACE. You know, that girl just... wasn't thinking... I think people are... people are interested in you and some people don't know how to... help *(Reaching out to him, touching his hair)* Some people get/ involved in a situation because they need to feel like they can...

KENNY. Don't. *(beat)* Stop. *(beat)* Stop it.

*(**KENNY** pushes her away hard. He is angry.)*

KENNY. Don't look at me. I don't like how you look at me.

GRACE. How do you even know how I look at you./ You don't...

*(**LAUREN** enters, unseen by **KENNY** and **GRACE** momentarily. She's dressed for the dance and holding a button down shirt in her hand.)*

KENNY. *(angry)* Just... Get away from me.

GRACE. I'm nowhere near you.

(They stand there. **LAUREN** *walks up to* **KENNY**. *Hands him the shirt.)*

LAUREN. You should wear this. Over your t-shirt. *(Her phone beeps. She flips it open)* God! I knew he was going to fucking do this. Seriously. 25 minutes early. *(Looks at the phone. Reading.)* I'm seven blocks away so I'll be there in under one minute.

*(***CAROLINE*** enters, wearing a skirt and t-shirt.)*

LAUREN. Whatever. He can drive us around for a while. I'm not being early to something I didn't want to go to in the first place. *(beat. To* **CAROLINE***)* So. Are you ready?

CAROLINE. Yeah, I'm ready. Hey your hair looks different.

LAUREN. *(exiting)* I brushed it.

*(***KENNY*** *puts the shirt on as he follows them wordlessly out the door.* **GRACE** *is alone in the kitchen with two unfinished glasses of milk sitting on the table. After another moment of cleaning up she sits, takes a sip of the milk. Sits. Looks at it. Then she deliberately pours the milk onto the floor in a slow, steady stream. Lights fade.)*

THE POLICE STATION

(Early evening. **OFFICER STEVENS**, *a police officer, sits at his desk, filling out paperwork.* **GRACE** *sits next to him watching.)*

GRACE. Did you always want to be a cop?

STEVENS. My dad was a cop. My brothers are both cops.

GRACE. So they wouldn't have supported your being, say, a dancer. Or a pastry chef.

STEVENS. I don't know. I always figured it'd go this way.

GRACE. Have you ever shot anyone?

STEVENS. No ma'am. I haven't.

GRACE. Ma'am. How old am I? How old does it say I am there?

STEVENS. You're forty-one.

GRACE. That's true. That's completely true. *(beat)* The bathrooms here are really nice.

STEVENS. They were renovated. Those improvements have an impact on workplace morale.

GRACE. Oh. You don't really buy that do you?

STEVENS. No I don't.

*(DANIEL *runs in.)*

DANIEL. God! Are you alright? I got home and our house… and everything was… and I didn't know what happened and then the neighbors told me you/ were here and I…

GRACE. Oh! Officer Stevens, this is my husband, Daniel.

DANIEL. Are you okay?

GRACE. Yes. Where were you?

DANIEL. What?

GRACE. You. Where were you all day?

DANIEL. Grocery. Car Wash. Dry Cleaning. *(pause)* And I… uh, I went to a movie.

GRACE. You went to/ a movie?

DANIEL. Okay, goddammit, I went to two movies. In a row. By myself. And I didn't pay for the second one.

GRACE. *(beat. To* STEVENS.*)* And he used to steal.

DANIEL. *(To* STEVENS*)* I needed a break.

STEVENS. Sir. You should know your wife's being held here on disturbing the peace and destruction of city and personal property. You should probably get a lawyer if assault charges are filed. But it's nothing that should amount to more than some pretty heavy fines.

GRACE. That was very official.

STEVENS. I've been doing this for a while.

DANIEL. I'm sorry, would you be able to give us a minute? Get her some water?

STEVENS. *(beat.)* Sure. I'll get it.

*(*STEVENS *exits.)*

GRACE. I'm sorry/... I...

DANIEL. Who did you assault?!

GRACE. I don't know his name/ but it wasn't...

DANIEL. You assaulted a man?

GRACE. I didn't intend to assault anyone. I was trying to help. While you were on your break, I was trying to help everyone. I walked into the kitchen and Kenny's in there with Kate, his mentor, practicing his speech. And he's standing up completely straight. Looking out. Do you know how long it's been since I've seen him stand like that? It was going so well. But she's like all the other people keeping him at a distance. And I wanted to kill her. I was so angry I probably could have... And I tried to touch him and really, he barely looks at me. He'll look at Caroline. He'll look at Lauren. He'll look right at you. But he won't look at me. And then they left for the dance and I was sitting in the kitchen alone and I... I couldn't be in that house anymore, I couldn't be in there so I walked outside to get some air and calm down. And those gardeners were finishing replanting next door after that pipe burst and they were packing up. So I walked over to check in with Bonnie, see if everything was alright and I see this man, one of the gardeners on our lawn. He was hiding in the bushes on the side of the house. And his pants were down. And he was going to the bathroom. On my lawn. On our lawn.

DANIEL. Jesus… Grace… .

GRACE. He's outside, exposed, on my lawn, quietly shitting on
my lawn, like it wasn't anything, like this was something
he did all the time, like crouching behind a hydranga
bush made him invisible. And I ran over there screaming, I was screaming, and you know I can really scream,
you've never actually heard me scream. It's so loud.
Shocked the hell out of me. And I ran up to him and
I kicked him. Hard. Right in the ankle. All the time…
screaming and screaming. I guess all the other women
in the neighborhood turn a blind eye because his face…
He looked so surprised. And I started hitting him with
my hands and I grabbed his shirt and pushed him down
and put his face right near his mess and I said, you're
going to clean that up, you don't shit on people's lawns.
Who do you think you are? I live here. My family lives
here. And he started crying, saying something I couldn't
understand, full of shame and anger. And then I started
crying, apologizing to him over and over so now we're
both there. Sobbing. And that was when I went back
inside and I started throwing everything away. I'd see
something and I'd pick it up, take it outside and drop
it at the curb. Plates, furniture, pictures, all your clothes.
And then I knocked down the mailbox. And that was
really satisfying so I knocked down the Kirschenbaum's
mailbox across the street. Then… well then the police
came over. And brought me here. That's what happened
to me. How was your day? What happened to you?

(STEVENS *returns with the water. Hands it to* GRACE.)

DANIEL. Can I take her home/ now?

GRACE. I don't want to go home.

DANIEL. I'll clean everything up. Come on.

GRACE. All of it? Even if I don't want to have a baby?

DANIEL. Can we talk about this/ later?

GRACE. No. When I go home and see what I did to the
house, I'm going to feel awful and I'll try and make
you feel better. I won't do it.

DANIEL. Okay.

GRACE. Never. I'll never get pregnant and have another baby. I won't./ I won't ever have another child.

DANIEL. I got it, okay.

GRACE. You're never going to look at kid and see yourself or your nose or your eyes. And maybe you'll have parts of Lauren and Kenny, maybe more of them over time but I can't guarantee anything. But you'll have me. I just... I need to be clear.

DANIEL. Yeah. *(beat)* Yeah. That's very clear.

GRACE. Is it?

DANIEL. Alright, so, uhm, do I owe you any money? Bail or do I need to give you a credit card or something?

GRACE. No, I'm not ready to go back there. *(To* **STEVENS***)* Can I go to jail?

DANIEL. You're not going to jail./ Don't be ridiculous.

GRACE. *(Ignoring him. To* **STEVENS***)* Let me ask you a practical question. What would you do if I had nowhere to go. If I didn't have a family. You couldn't force me out onto the street until tomorrow morning, could you? You'd have to hold me overnight. *(beat)* Please.

STEVENS. Why don't I help you to the bathroom, you can wash your face, there's a couch in back. You can catch your breath and then we'll see where you want to go.

GRACE. Okay. I'm not interested in compromises right now but okay.

STEVENS. I'll keep that in mind. *(he offers her his hand and helps her up.)*

(They start to walk away.)

GRACE. You need to pick Kenny up at the dance. He's going to call when he wants a ride home. So you'll/ have to...

DANIEL. I'll get him. *(beat)* It's good that he went.

GRACE. *(A pause)* He looked so nice.

*(***DANIEL*** nods. ***GRACE*** exits with ***STEVENS***. ***DANIEL*** stands in the police station before exiting.)*

THE DANCE

(*Bad music starts up. Colored lights swirl on the floor and paper decorations fall into view.* **CHARLIE** *and* **LAUREN** *next to* **KENNY** *and* **CAROLINE**. *They stand watching other people dance with trepidation. All except for* **CHARLIE**.)

CHARLIE. So. Do you want to dance?

LAUREN. To this?

CHARLIE. You're right. It's bad. We'll wait for the next one.

KENNY. Do we have to/dance...

CAROLINE. Of course not. Not unless you want to? Do you/ want to?

KENNY. I don't think so./ Not right now.

CAROLINE. Alright.

CHARLIE. (*Reaching in his jacket pockets*) Oh. Hey, I brought you something.

LAUREN. (*Squeezing her eyes closed. Mortified.*) Oh. God. Not a corsage.

CHARLIE. No. And it's not for you. (*Hands Kenny a CD*)

KENNY. Songs With Kick Ass Saxophone. Volume One.

CHARLIE. Oh and Track 5 is this Sting song "Englishman in New York" which I only put on there as an example of how sometimes it's better to go with an oboe than a saxophone but that's not usually the case. I go into more detail in the liner notes.

KENNY. ...Thanks.

CHARLIE. Yeah dude, no problem.

(**LAUREN** *looks out at the dance floor. Nearly smiles, she can't help it.*)

LAUREN. C'mon. This song is definitely bearable.

CHARLIE. Really? Wow, okay, honestly, I didn't think you were going to actually dance with me. At all. Really?

LAUREN. Well do you not/ want to now?

CHARLIE. (*Grabbing her hand and pulling her out there*) Nonono, let's go!

(*He pulls her out to the dance floor.* **CAROLINE** *and*

KENNY *watch as lights fade slightly on them.)*

CHARLIE. Hey. Did you know I can do the... *(he does a dance move).*

LAUREN. *(Not impressed)* Wow. The only thing I can do are impressions.

CHARLIE. Really?

LAUREN. Yeah. Guess who I am. *(Imitating Charlie)* I really like this song. It's good. I mean it's slow. But a good sort of slow, kinda fast/slow so there's still enough going on that you can move around. Sometimes I like a good slow song. I mean, it's different than a fast song. Because it's, you know, slower.

CHARLIE. You know what I think this means?

LAUREN. It means you're annoying and have an annoying way of speaking.

CHARLIE. Or maybe. It means. You love me.

LAUREN. I don't.

CHARLIE. Well, I think you do. A little.

LAUREN. You think I love you a little?

CHARLIE. You hate me. You hate the way I talk. You hate the songs I write for you. Your brother and Aunt came with us on our first date. Yeah, I think you love me a lot.

(They dance)

CHARLIE. You want to kiss me?

LAUREN. No. I don't. *(beat)* Stop looking at me like that.

CHARLIE. C'mon. You already love me. And now. We kiss.

LAUREN. That's stupid.

CHARLIE. Really? I think it's pretty standard.

LAUREN. Now if I kiss you I automatically love you?

CHARLIE. Yeah. Sorry. *(In a robot voice)* Automatic love.

LAUREN. ...*(Horrified by his nerd robot voice)*

CHARLIE. You're not going to kiss me?

LAUREN. No.

CHARLIE. Okay. *(He leans over, about to kiss her.)* You sure?

LAUREN. Yes. *(They kiss. A pause)*

CHARLIE. How was that?

LAUREN. So you want to have sex?

CHARLIE. *(beat)* Umm... No?/Right now? No.

LAUREN. But you want to.

CHARLIE. Yeah, like in the grand scheme of /things, sure but...

LAUREN. It's okay if that's what you want but I think you should just be straightforward/ and put your sex cards on the table.

CHARLIE. Should I have used my tongue/ or something?

LAUREN. Look, I'd just like to know. Obviously I'm cool with it.

CHARLIE. I don't know...

LAUREN. You do know. Everyone knows.

CHARLIE. No I mean... I know. But. You don't talk to any of those guys now. I mean, I don't see you talking to any of those guys unless you're calling them on your own time or whatever. But you don't hang out with any of them. So. I don't know.

(A slow song begins. They notice. After a beat, reluctantly, LAUREN and CHARLIE start to dance as lights fade on them slightly and rise on CAROLINE and KENNY watching people dance. CAROLINE looks at KENNY who has just started to sway to the song.)

CAROLINE. Are you dancing.

KENNY. What?

CAROLINE. You were going like this. *(Sways along to the song)*

KENNY. No I /wasn't.

CAROLINE. Do you want to dance?

KENNY. No.

CAROLINE. One song.

KENNY. ...No. I don't/ want to.

CAROLINE. None of these kids can dance. Look at them.

KENNY. No. Okay? I don't want to. Stop asking me.

CAROLINE. Alright.

KENNY. I... I hate this place. They try to dress it up. It's the cafeteria. I hate the cafeteria. I hate these people.

CAROLINE. Why? What did they do?

KENNY. *(Shuts off.)* Nothing.

(**KENNY** *will not look at her.*)

CAROLINE. What did they do to you?

KENNY. I don't know. They were mean.

CAROLINE. How were they mean?

KENNY. Mean. I don't know.

CAROLINE. Well. People are mean, man. There are really terrible mean people out there so you better learn how to deal with them. (**KENNY** *looks away, annoyed. With force, now.*) Hey! Tell me what they did to you. Tell me.

KENNY. They forgot my name.

CAROLINE. They forgot your name? *(a beat)* And. That's all?

KENNY. ...They... forgot my name. On purpose. It was... funny to them everytime I had to reintroduce myself. I'd... I'd walk over to, uh, sit down with people at lunch and they'd pretend they didn't know who I was, or they'd say Hi Kevin. And I'd say Kenny and they'd laugh. The guys made me write it on my papers, or they'd write it on my papers, tell my teachers I'd changed my name, so they'd call me something different in class. Kevin. Korey. Kelly. Karen. And I thought they'd stop but then they didn't. The girls mostly laughed and made fun of my drawings. They did it every time they saw me. Every single day. All the time. They never got tired of it they liked it that much.

CAROLINE. And how is it now?

KENNY. They don't talk to me. They know who I am. *(beat)* I've gotta apologize. To all of them. On Monday. And I can't swear when I do it. *(beat)* Will you still be here? Next week?

(**CAROLINE** *looks around.* **CHARLIE** *and* **LAUREN** *are still dancing.*)

CAROLINE. I don't think /I can....

KENNY. Mom, Daniel and Lauren are going to sit in the front row while I say it to everyone. Will you stay?

CAROLINE. *(Very gently)* I have to figure out where I'm going next.*

KENNY. Yeah... Or. Can I come?

CAROLINE. Where?

KENNY. You know, when you go... wherever you're going. Can I come?

CAROLINE. *(Pause. Putting her hands on his shoulders)* Listen, I'll make you a promise. Alright? I promise you that soon, you will be older. *(beat)* You will.

(She takes his hands and puts them on her waist and puts her hands back on his shoulders so he is now slow-dancing with her, like it or not.)

CAROLINE. See... Now, when you decide to dance with girls, girls your own age, you should stand up straight. Girls dance a closer when you stand up straighter. You can talk through the verses but look right at them on the chorus.

KENNY. Okay. *(beat)* Can we call my mom to pick us up/ now?

CAROLINE. Absolutely.

(They exit. LAUREN and CHARLIE still dancing.)

LAUREN. Do you want to go?

CHARLIE. No. Do you?

LAUREN. Uh, I guess. People are starting to take off. And this song is awful.

CHARLIE. It's not/awful.

LAUREN. Charlie. This song is bullshit. You could write a better song than this.

CHARLIE. Yeah?

LAUREN. *(beat)* Yeah, okay? But I could probably write a better song too. So don't get all thrilled.

THE CAR

(Lights up on DANIEL *and* CAROLINE *in the car outside the campgrounds.)*

CAROLINE. Thanks for picking us up. *(beat)* Hey? You okay?

DANIEL. Yeah, yeah, I'm fine. So are you going to head back to your tent? I have to go back home and clean up... everything.

CAROLINE. *(Going into her daypack)* You want to smoke a bowl?

DANIEL. I know it feels like you just went back in time but you do realize you're not actually back in high school.

CAROLINE. C'mon. Roll up the windows.

DANIEL. No. I can't.

CAROLINE. Dude. I've spent the evening surrounded by teenagers and fake palm trees. It's been a rough night for everyone.

DANIEL. *(Angry)* You think I don't want to get really stoned? I do. I'm fun, okay? But nothing's... working. I mean, I sat alone in a movie theater for almost five hours and I couldn't relax. All I do is think about all of them. I just worry about him and I think about how she's... That's what I do now. All the time.

CAROLINE. God, you must wonder how you ended up here.

DANIEL. Where? No I/ don't.

CAROLINE. C'mon. You don't walk around that house every day and think, "How did I get here?"

DANIEL. I don't have that kind of free time.

CAROLINE. Look. I mean, of course you're freaking out. You have a meaningless job, your kids don't like you, your house is destroyed, your wife is in jail.

DANIEL. It sounds fucking awful when you put it that way.

CAROLINE. Isn't it?

DANIEL. No. Not really. *(beat)* It's not like they're going to appreciate it right now. Okay? But at least now they actually need me around. They don't like me? Fine. Fine. They can not like me while I make them lunch and drive them around and listen to them and then we can fight and watch t.v. and eat dinner. All together. And then we can go to bed and wake up and do it all over again. That's what I want. And one day they will like me for that. One day they will love me for that, I think.

(She looks at him)

CAROLINE. Thank you for the ride.

DANIEL. Sure. *(a beat)* Do you think I should go back there and get them?

CAROLINE. They'll be fine. Honestly, they're at a police station.

DANIEL. I know. I just want everyone at home.

THE POLICE STATION

(Lights up stage right, the police station. STEVENS is sitting as a desk. KENNY walks in, looks around.)

STEVENS. *(Barks)* Hey!/HEY! You're not supposed to be back here.

KENNY. Oh. The... /uh...

STEVENS. Stop there. You can't walk/ back here.

KENNY. The officer out front said/ to...

STEVENS. Said to just wander on through? Have look around? *(KENNY walks over to him.)* Shouldn't there be an adult with you?

KENNY. I, uh, there is. There were. My aunt and stepdad drove me here. And/ my mom is... Is my mom here?

STEVENS. *(beat)* Yeah. She is.

KENNY. May I... see her?

STEVENS. She's resting in the back room.

KENNY. Oh. Okay. Can I wait? I...

(He sits)

STEVENS. Your family planning anything else I should know about? Your sister pulling a bank job soon?

KENNY. ...No...

STEVENS. Well, I will say. Your mom is a very polite lady. Much better manners than you when we brought you in here.

KENNY. Yeah. I don't... remember what/ happened...

STEVENS. You don't remember kicking people before we had you restrained. Before we got you under control. You knocked over everything on my desk. You broke a mug my son painted for.

KENNY. *(Upset)* I did.

STEVENS. Yeah.

KENNY. I... If I had remembered that, I would... *(Pause)* I don't really remember a lot of that day. ...I wish I hadn't broken your mug.

(A pause.)

STEVENS. How's school?

KENNY. It's hard.

STEVENS. *(beat)* So, you want to talk to her?

KENNY. Yeah.

STEVENS. Just wait here.

> (**STEVENS** *walks out to get* **GRACE.** **KENNY** *waits there.*
> *Looks around.* **STEVENS** *walks in with* **GRACE**)

KENNY. …Mom?

GRACE. Oh. *(beat)* How was the dance? Did you have fun?
Did you dance?

KENNY. Not really. *(beat)* Yeah. But not like, well.

(A beat.)

STEVENS. Look, I've gotta go teach that lifeguard out front
what it means to be a cop. You got her under control?

KENNY. …What?

STEVENS. It's a joke.

GRACE. *(beat)* Oh. That was/ good.

STEVENS. No it/ wasn't.

GRACE. No. That was funny.

STEVENS. Alright.

> (**STEVENS** *exits.*
>
> *A pause.)*

GRACE. Where's your sister?

KENNY. Still dancing. With this guy.

GRACE. Really?

KENNY. Yeah… He won't let her leave til the very end.

GRACE. Is he cute?

KENNY. I don't know. He's nice, I guess. *(beat)* He was really
nice

GRACE. To you? (**KENNY** *nods.)* Good.

(A pause.)

KENNY. So do you /want to… .

GRACE. I want to stay right here.

KENNY. What are we going to do here?/There's nothing to do.

GRACE. I have no idea. I just want to sit here for a while.

KENNY. Okay… How long are/ you…

GRACE. Maybe through the weekend

KENNY. Are you allowed to do that?

GRACE. I don't know.

KENNY. Okay… I'll stay too.

GRACE. Oh. *(Pause)* Alright.

> *(She moves over to make some room and he sits down next to her. They sit there together.*
>
> *A pause)*

GRACE. Can I…

KENNY. What?

GRACE. *(A beat. She's very unsure of how to begin with him)* That day… when they brought you here. After/ they…

KENNY. I know. *(Pause)* What.

GRACE. And I said… I said I'd never /forgive…

KENNY. Yeah, We don't have to/ talk about…

GRACE. Listen to me, it's/ not…

KENNY. Whatever, okay, /I don't…

GRACE. God, you make me so nervous you stupid kid.

> *(pause)*

GRACE. Kenny, look… it's… not… I'm not good at forgiving anyone. Or, I don't know, I've never been able to do it fast enough. It takes me such long time… Which is not a good quality, I'm not saying it's a good quality. But… I remember, when you were little, I'd stand and watch you play. And I could see how you took everything so hard, harder than the other kids. You noticed everything, I wish you didn't but you did and you felt…
> We're a terrible fit. I don't know if you'll ever find your place. I mean, I haven't…

KENNY. I'm... I'm sorry that/ I...

GRACE. I know. I see your face every day. I know you are. *(A pause.* **GRACE** *looks around the room.)* I wonder how many people we know have actually done time in here.

KENNY. Yeah.

GRACE. Probably none.

KENNY. *(pause)* Well. Mrs. Armstrong. *(beat)* That time they thought she kidnapped that kid Scottie.

GRACE. You remember that? You were 7.

KENNY. Yeah. *(beat)* You said if I saw a strange unmarked van to start screaming "Fire!" and run towards someone/ I thought I knew.

GRACE. That's right.

KENNY. Yeah. *(beat)* And then I had all those dreams about like... sinister minivans. And fires.

GRACE. You did?

KENNY. Yeah. And then Dad got you a minivan...

GRACE. God, I hated that car.

KENNY. Yeah.

GRACE. I really did. *(A pause)* I keep having this dream about breakfast.

KENNY. Like about food?

GRACE. Yeah. I have it at least once a week. In the dream, I wake up and I come downstairs and you and Lauren are arguing because you took the last bagel. And I yell at both of you for fighting over food because it's ridiculous, there's cereal, there's yogurt, there are a million other things you can eat for breakfast. So we're all sitting there and I'm aggravated and your sister's slamming cabinets shut. And you're standing there. Standing on the counter, eating a bagel. And you're not sorry at all. *(She smiles.)*

KENNY. C'mon. *(She doesn't get up)* Mom... Get up. Please. We've gotta go home.

*(**KENNY** carefully touches **GRACE** on the shoulder. Lights fade slightly on **GRACE** and **KENNY** who stay where they*

are. Lights rise stage left on **LAUREN** *and* **CHARLIE,** *still slow dancing.)*

LAUREN. There's no more music. We look like idiots.

CHARLIE. I'm having the best time.

(They dance)

CHARLIE. Don't you want to stay? Right here. Like this.

LAUREN. You're really tall. I need to put my arms down. C'mon.

CHARLIE. But, tomorrow the cafeteria will just be the cafeteria. We'll look around and it won't look like this and it won't feel like this and…

LAUREN. Dude. Tomorrow's Saturday. We can go see a movie or something.

(Lights out.)

THE POSTCARD/THE APOLOGY

(Lights up on **KENNY**, *standing on a platform center stage. A microphone stands a few feet in front of him. The sound of students chattering grows and then fades. We see* **GRACE**, **DANIEL** *and* **LAUREN** *sitting in the front row [facing the audience] downstage left.* **KENNY** *walks up to the microphone his speech in hand.* **CAROLINE** *steps into a spotlight downstage right.)*

CAROLINE. Kenny. I'm leaving you this picture of Everest. I didn't take it, I bought it off this guy I met who just got back from his third trek. It doesn't make up for taking off without saying goodbye but still it's a pretty unreal picture, isn't it. The crazy thing is, this guy took it right after he fell 400 feet. He told me when he landed and realized he wasn't dead, he got out his camera, laid flat on his back and took a picture. This is what it looks like, way up there right after you fall. Lying on your back, looking straight up, holding on. Can you imagine it?

(They both stand there. Nervous. Unsure. They all take a breath. Then, an enormous gust of wind blows and before they can exhale or start to speak… Blackout.)

End of Play